Sofi Keren

2019

Bella Books, Inc.
P.O. Box 10543
Tallahassee, FL 32302

Printed in the United States of America on acid-free paper.

First Bella Books Edition 2019

Editor: Ann Roberts
Cover Designer: Sandy Knowles

ISBN: 978-1-64247-066-6

About the Author

Sofi Keren lives in upstate New York, where she chases waterfalls, writes stories, and makes long to-do lists that she will never finish. Originally from Indianapolis, she embraces her nostalgia by setting many of her stories there. *Painted Over* is her debut novel.

Acknowledgments

When I was a little kid, I said I was going to write books when I grew up. My family never doubted that for a minute, even if sometimes I did. Thank you to my parents, my sisters, and your dudes, who have always loved and accepted me for who I am. I know how lucky I am to have you. Your support, encouragement, and terrible dad jokes mean the world to me.

Stephanie, my writing partner in crime, thank you for believing in me for the last many years and reading all my stories, some much better than others. Sarah, so much love to you for all your pep talks and support while I went through the writer life cycle of loving-hating-loving my work.

Melissa and Chris, thank you for always being in my corner. MaryAnna, my self-appointed PR person and constant cheerleader, you are a wonderful human being. Stacey, Jeremy, Kristin, Britnee, I'm so fortunate to have had the opportunity to work with you. Sorry I up and moved away but we'll always have Slack. Kelly, and Bethany, you've been lifesavers to me and I love you for it. Carmen, Phyllis, and Sue, I miss you like hell but please do not save me any squash this year. Erin and Nick, I love you and miss your faces. Greg, you better come visit me. Thank you to my writing groups for making me a better writer and supporting me on this crazy path. To all my amazing friends who give me so much love and support, I'm so fortunate to have you in my life and you're all very attractive. Thank you for letting me be my total weirdo self with you.

Thank you to my editor, Ann Roberts, for all your thoughtful feedback. This book is light years ahead of its early self because of you. Thank you to Jessica and all of the staff at Bella Books for believing in me and this book.

Thank you to you, the person reading these words right now. I'm honored to have your eyes on these pages. Thank you for spending your time with me.

Dedication

To Indianapolis, the city I love no matter
where I lay my head.

CHAPTER ONE

Paige saw the light turn yellow, but she knew she could make it through. She willed the wheels of her bike to turn faster. Speeding through the intersection, legs pumping, she just avoided a Kia making a last-minute left turn.

"Damn cyclists! Watch where you're going!" a man's voice boomed as the Kia sped off. Paige simply raised her middle finger in his general direction and kept pedaling. After all, technically the right of way had been hers. Her blond ponytail levitated behind her as the breeze pushed lightly against her momentum. *Finally, a beautiful day.* She'd been waiting for April's gray gloominess to pass and finally May had officially kicked it to the curb.

She knew she should be in her studio, working on the commissioned pieces that would pay her rent for the next few months, but there was no way she could be inside when the weather was so perfect. She wasn't alone. Along Mass Ave all the restaurants with outdoor seating were overflowing. Everyone in Indianapolis must be playing hooky from work today. She sat upright on her seat, enjoying the feel of sunshine on her shoulders.

Looking around her at the city come alive, she took her eyes off the road for just a moment. But it was long enough for her front wheel to catch in a giant pothole that seemed to appear out of nowhere. The bike wobbled dangerously beneath her.

"Fucking hell!" she yelled on her way down.

Sprawled on the pavement, she assessed the damage part by part. As far as she could tell, she was all right, though her heart was beating like a hummingbird's wings. There was a big dirty smudge on her favorite jeans, but she seemed otherwise unscathed. Her bike fared worse; its tire clearly flat, the rim bent. *Damn it.* Inconvenient, but at least it was fixable. And of course today of all days she didn't have her patch kit with her.

Paige stood and stretched, waving away the well-meaning onlookers. Why were there always witnesses whenever she did something embarrassing? She could walk the bike home, but that would take forever. It was a simple repair really, and there was one other option. The CycleWorthy bike shop was only a couple blocks away. She hesitated. She hadn't been there in forever, with good reason. But thinking of Mr. Worth, she smiled. It wasn't his fault she'd exiled herself from the family. She missed him, and surely he would be happy to see her. She headed toward the shop.

The front door of CycleWorthy was unlocked, but no one seemed to be around. Typical, she thought. Mr. Worth was always leaving the front room and all its gear unattended while he worked on bikes in the back. She admired his trusting nature, but she worried that someone would take advantage of it someday. Indianapolis wasn't New York, but it wasn't a small town either.

Wheels and bike frames of all styles hung on the walls and from the ceiling. Paige found herself ogling the brightly colored ones. She'd always been tempted to choose her bike parts based on looks over function. She liked to believe that was because she was an artist, not because she was a magpie, attracted to bright and shiny objects.

Paige leaned her wounded bike carefully against the counter and thumbed through one of the many cycling magazines stacked up on it. After waiting a few minutes, she tapped the bell sitting next to the register.

She heard the rustle as someone emerged from the back room.

"What do you think?" she asked without looking up from her article. "Should I ride my bike across Siberia like this lady?"

"I don't know. It sounds pretty cold to me," a woman's voice replied.

Paige dropped the magazine and looked up. The woman stood there grinning, a mischievous smile playing across her lips, her golden brown eyes twinkling. A striped racer-back tank top showed off her muscled arms, sculpted from years of athletics. Her dark hair stood up in that trademark faux-mohawk of hers. Paige saw reflections in her features of both her Filipina mother and her farm-bred Iowan father. She was a little older now, her features a little less soft, but Paige still lost her breath at the sight of her.

"Ria," Paige said, her voice scratchy like she'd nearly lost it. She coughed. "What are you... I mean, you're home. I hadn't heard."

"I just got in yesterday. Thought I'd come into the shop today to hang out with Dad. He just ran out to get coffee."

As if on cue, the door chimed and Henry Worth pushed his way in, balancing two very large plastic-capped cups of coffee in his hands. He sported a scruffy beard laced through with gray that was new since she'd seen him last. "Paige! What a treat!"

"Hey, Mr. Worth," she said shyly.

"Mr. Worth?" He laughed. "When did you stop calling me Henry?"

"Sorry, Henry."

"So, two of my favorite ladies in one place—my star athlete and our very own local Van Gogh . To what do I owe the honor?"

"The fact that they still haven't paved over all those potholes on Mass Ave yet, unfortunately."

"Well, whatever the reason, it's good to see you. Now let's take a look." Setting the coffee on the counter, he knelt down to inspect the offending tire. "Oh yeah, it really bit you. All right, bring it on back and Ria will get you taken care of."

"Oh I will, will I?"

"I know you can't be that rusty, Ria. You may spend most of your time kicking soccer balls around, but I know I taught you a thing or two about the family business."

"You mean writing romance novels? I'm afraid I just don't have the talent."

He laughed. "I think your mother has enough writing talent for the whole family. I'll stick to my bike arts and parts. Now let's get Paige fixed up."

"Oh, you really don't have to," Paige interjected. "If I can borrow some tools I can do it myself, no problem."

"It's no problem at all," Ria said. "I've got you." She came around to Paige's side of the counter. Paige handed off the bike, and as she did, Ria's fingers brushed across her hand. Paige's heart thumped and she immediately told herself to knock it off. They'd been friends since they were kids. And then they weren't. There was nothing to get so undone about. But she couldn't help but wonder, was that an accident? Not that it mattered. All that was in the past, buried for years.

Ria rolled the bike behind the counter and removed the offending wheel and then pulled off the tire. Placing the wheel on a truing stand, she checked the spokes and tightened them where necessary. Paige stood awkwardly off to one side and watched.

"So, how's everything?"

"Oh," Ria replied, "always interesting. I hear things are going well for you."

"You do?"

"Oh yeah, you know Mom. She keeps track of everything. Sends me links when there are articles about you in the paper. I think she has a Google Alert set on your name."

Paige laughed. "Sounds like your mom. How is she doing?"

"She's great. Just published another book. Hold on a sec. Dad, can you toss me a new tube?"

Once satisfied that the wheel was straight and steady, Ria expertly slid on the tube, replaced the tire, and inflated it to the right pressure. She always made everything look so easy.

Henry walked over to take a look and gave an approving smile. "She's still got it."

"Thanks, Dad. Glad to know I still have a backup if this soccer thing doesn't work out."

"You laugh, but you know someday I'm going to retire."

"Sure you are, Dad, sure you are."

He wheeled the bike back around to the front. "All fixed up and almost as good as new."

Paige dug her wallet out of her bag and started to open it, but Henry just laughed and held up his hand. "Oh, please. Your money is no good here."

"You don't need to do that," Paige protested, shifting uncomfortably.

"Don't be silly," Henry insisted. "You know we do repairs for the family all the time. And you might not be blood but you're certainly family."

"Speaking of family," he continued, "we're having a big get-together tomorrow night. I'm so glad you wandered in so I could invite you. It'll give you and Ria a chance to catch up, since she's never home."

"Daaaaaad," Ria protested. "You know it's not that I don't *want* to come home."

"I know. I'm only kidding." He gave Ria a quick kiss on the head. "Paige, will you join us? I know Mila would love to see you, not to mention the rest of the family."

"Oh I don't know," Paige said, caught by surprise. "I don't want to intrude."

"Since when have you been an intruder?" He laughed. "We've known each other since before I had any of this glorious gray hair. You probably still have a key somewhere. You know that our house is your house."

Paige looked up at Ria, trying to read her expression, but as usual, Ria kept her thoughts to herself.

After what seemed like forever, but was probably only a moment, Ria added, "Please come. It's been a long time."

How long had it been now? Twelve, maybe thirteen years? And if it hadn't been for the flat tire, it could have been forever. Paige hadn't realized until now just how much she'd missed the family. Maybe it was a sign that it was time to move on, to finally let it go. Carrying around all that ancient hurt and anger wasn't helping anyone, and if Ria could get past it, then maybe so could she.

CHAPTER TWO

"Maybe I could pretend to be sick," Paige said to her roommate, Brandon, who was perched on a stool next to her at the kitchen counter. "Food poisoning is always a good excuse. It comes on quickly so there wouldn't be any surprise that I seemed fine yesterday. Or a migraine maybe?"

Brandon raised one eyebrow at her and continued eating his lunch without comment.

"Okay, okay, I know that's stupid. Maybe I could just go for an hour and then sneak out the back? Do an Irish goodbye?"

"As a person of Irish descent, I'm extremely offended that you think that's how we leave each other, just sneaking out the back without a word."

"I am so sorry, Brandon. Please share my apologies with your ancestors."

"Thank you. So why is it that you can't just go and be social? What's the big deal about this again?"

"It's a long story. We had…kind of a falling out in college, and we haven't spoken since. But before that we were basically inseparable since we were little."

"I see. Well that makes sense. You should definitely hold a grudge over some old fight from a million years ago instead of making up with your childhood friend. That sounds like a good life choice."

Paige scowled. "It's more complicated than that."

"Isn't it always? What's this girl's name again?"

"Ria. I've talked about her before, I'm sure. She plays soccer. Like, World Cup-level soccer."

Brandon spun around on his stool. "Hold up. Excuse me, are you talking about Pride-of-Indianapolis soccer star Ria? Even I know who that is and I hate sports. And so do you, come to think of it."

"Yeah, that Ria."

He hooted. "Well that explains a lot."

"It does?"

"Um. Yes. Now I get why you're always watching soccer games on your laptop. Even the ones no one cares about because, let's just be honest, the only ones worth watching are the World Cup and maybe the Olympics."

"That's not true!" She swatted at him. "It's a good game! I played when I was little, you know. I just like watching it."

"Uh huh. Sure. Now it all makes sense. You are *such* a stalker." He took a bite of the massive sandwich in front of him.

"It's not stalking if the games are streaming on the internet. They're public!"

He laughed. "A little defensive, are we?"

"You know, you wouldn't have to eat so much if you worked out less. You'd cut your grocery bill in half. And your T-shirts wouldn't be so damn tight."

"My T-shirts are just the right amount of tight. And don't change the subject."

"It's just…it's not like that."

"Of course not. But you're going, right? To this party thing?"

"You really don't understand."

"You're going."

"Fine. I'm going. Happy?"

"Deliriously. But promise me something."

"What."

"If there's cake, bring me home a piece. Maybe two."

Paige sat in her car in the Worths' driveway, looking up at the house. The Worth home had always seemed so huge. Now that she was older and taller, it was less imposing, but it still managed to look stately without being ostentatious.

If the Worths had wanted, they easily could have owned one of those sprawling mega-mansions so common to certain pockets of the Carmel suburbs. By comparison, the five-bedroom cottage was downright charming.

As she pulled into the long winding drive, it felt like going back in time. If she looked down, she could almost imagine seeing her favorite old overalls or the giant-legged jeans she'd constructed out of thrift store finds in high school to mimic the popular but whoa-too-expensive JNCO brand. She'd buy two pairs of jeans at Goodwill, slice one pair up the side, and sew in extra denim to achieve a similar effect. Luckily DIY punk was a thing, and she looked grungy and intentional instead of broke. Nowadays she was more into skinny jeans that wouldn't get trapped in her bike chain.

Paige lingered in the parked car, not ready to get out and go inside just yet. For a moment she considered sneaking the car back down the drive and coming up with some convincing excuse for her absence, a last-minute consultation or a family thing with her dad. She wished for the hundredth time that she was a better liar. Mila had texted her last night saying, *We can't wait to see you!* Ria's mom was nothing if not relentless when she wanted something. The message made Paige smile, even though the thought of being in the same room as Ria and having to make small talk twisted her insides into knots—not to mention having to explain to everyone why she'd disappeared.

Sucking in a deep gulp of air, she readied herself and pushed the car door open, propelling herself in the direction of the house. She could hear music and voices coming from the backyard. Making her way around to the open gate, she could see the party was already in full swing.

The whole family was there. Ria's parents, Henry and Mila, held court on the patio, surrounded by all five of their now-grown kids and their partners. Everyone was older and paired off now, but Paige would know them anywhere.

She was surprised to see Jerald there. This must be a special occasion if Ria's big brother had traveled all the way from San Diego. Thanks to Facebook, Paige recognized the spouses and plus-ones, even though she hadn't met most of them in person. Several children,who Paige assumed belonged to Ria's sister Vina, played in a gazebo at the far corner of the yard.

Paige had always wanted to be a part of a big family, probably because hers was so small. Growing up with just her dad and no other extended family nearby, she'd been more than happy to let the Worths fill that need.

Looking out at the family, she tried to hold back tears. She hadn't realized how much she'd missed this. She hated that she'd lost over a decade with them. Maybe she shouldn't have been so stubborn. But what else could she have done?

She thought again of sneaking away, just taking a mental photo of the family and disappearing before things got weird. But just then, Ria's other sister, Amelia, saw her.

"Paige!" she called out warmly. Amelia greeted her and pushed the gate open further. Paige knelt down slightly to receive her hug from Amelia's four-foot-nine-inch frame. She may have been the smallest of the family, but Paige knew she'd become one of the fiercest lawyers in the city. She and her partners had their faces plastered on billboards all over the interstate.

"Hi, Amelia. It's so good to see you. You look wonderful." Amelia was clad in a rose print maxi dress and a huge statement necklace. All of a sudden Paige felt underdressed in her gray Dickies and light blue jersey top.

"It's about time you came to see us. I'm sure you're busy, but still. You know, we've all followed your career, but we want to hear all about it from you."

"Oh, no. You have to catch me up on all of you first."

"Well let's get you a drink, eh? Before Mom starts the interrogation."

Amelia swept her inside the party and immediately dispatched her husband to get drinks for all of them.

Mila loved any occasion for a party, and tonight was no different. Strings of lights hung between the trees, and music wafted through the air from the artfully concealed outdoor speaker system. Mila had always said if you were going to spend money, spend it on time with your loved ones.

Paige thought she was probably so generous with her money because she'd grown up with little of it. She'd always loved hearing Mila's stories about growing up in the Philippines. It all seemed so different, her life on the island, with no running water in the house for the first half of her life, the outdoor bathroom, and the mosquitos possibly bearing malaria. But Mila never complained. To her it was just life. And now that she was so fortunate, she made sure life was easier for her immediate family here, and her extended family back home. She had always promised to take them back home to visit when they were older, but Paige assumed she'd missed that chance now.

It would be easy to assume Henry was the one supporting the family. It was probably true for most of the families in the area, even if a little stereotypical. But the bike shop was more of a hobby than a career for him. It was Mila who supported the family. After she'd married Henry and come to America, she'd noticed all the paperback romance novels in the grocery store aisles and decided that she was going to have her name on ones right next to them. She bought all the books she could find, studied them as though she were cramming for an exam, and spent months writing an epic tale of love on two continents. Then she showed up at the publisher's address printed inside one of those books with her manuscript in hand, a risk that made other writers gasp when she told them about it. Somehow it had worked, probably in no small part due to her infectious enthusiasm. She'd convinced them to read the book, and they'd found a raw nugget of talent inside the pages. A year or so later, an enthusiastic review in People magazine had sent her debut novel shooting up the mass market bestseller list just a few rungs below Danielle Steele. Not that people knew it was her. The publisher had insisted she take a pseudonym. They didn't think Ermila Worth would sell as many copies as Gabrielle Mitchell.

As though she was called, Mila arrived at Paige's side and wrapped her in a warm hug. The woman barely seemed to have aged since Paige saw her last, though when she smiled, Paige thought she noticed a few faint new lines around her eyes. She knew Mila had been a beauty queen back home in the Philippines, and she could still see why.

"My fourth daughter," Mila said, squeezing her lightly. "Where have you been? We've missed you."

"I'm sorry, Mrs. Worth." Paige immediately felt thirteen again, as though she was about to get in trouble.

"It's okay, sweetheart. I know you'd been busy. I follow you on Instagram! So how is your father doing?"

"He's doing well, thank you. He and Celia just celebrated their third anniversary."

"That's wonderful. We should have them both over for dinner sometime. How is his health holding up?"

"You know, he's supposed to be working on his cholesterol, but he insists that life isn't worth living without some red meat. Celia replaces his hamburgers with veggie burgers when they go grocery shopping. They're both doing really well, even if he pretends to complain."

"I'm so glad to hear it. I've thought about him from time to time. Is he enjoying his retirement?"

"I think so. I think he misses negotiating deals over construction equipment—his work was so glamorous—but he keeps busy. He and Celia are even talking about buying an RV and becoming snowbirds."

Mila let out a peal of laughter. "I can't quite imagine your father as a tourist, but I am so glad he's happy. He certainly worked hard to give you a good life, and it's about time that he got to enjoy things and relax. I know how that is, now that we're empty nesters ourselves. Come, you have to see the rest of the family." Mila took her hand.

Paige knew saying no was not an option. Nearly dragging her across the yard, Mila deposited her in a semi-circle next to Jerald.

"I will be back soon. I have to check on my ham," Mila declared. "Catch up, all of you."

Mila was like that—a force of nature who blew in and out as she pleased.

"Hey Jerald," Paige said shyly. "It's good to see you."

"Paige!" he said with a smile. "You're so big." He hugged her tightly.

Paige laughed. Jerald had inherited his father's height and broad shoulders, with Paige coming up to just under his chin. She'd probably still been in junior high when he went off to Carnegie Mellon. He'd been kind of like a distant big brother. Sometimes he would drive Ria and her to soccer practice or the movies. And they'd known his big secret way before he'd dared to tell his parents he was gay. She remembered how scared he'd been that his ex-military dad would be angry, but it was his very Catholic mother that had taken some time to come around to the idea. He hadn't known it then, but he'd definitely paved the path so that it would be a little smoother when Ria was ready to come out herself.

"Oh, I'm being rude. Paige, this is my husband, Paul." Jerald indicated a slim, dapper, and slightly younger man sporting a classic red bowtie with his casual gray suit. "Paul, this is Paige, Ria's best friend. They were always running around underfoot, causing trouble." He winked at her and she smiled back.

"And Jer was always wandering around conducting imaginary orchestras. He'd get so embarrassed when we'd catch him. But look how it all worked out."

"It's great to meet you, Paige," Paul said, extending a hand.

They made an attractive couple. Jer (never Jerry) had grown into his looks from the awkward teenager she remembered. Of course she'd seen Mila's posts over the years, proudly telling the world about her son's achievements as he conducted all over the world before accepting a lucrative contract with the San Diego Orchestra.

"Where is Ria, anyway?" Jerald wondered out loud. "She's supposed to do the first toast for our parents. Can you believe they've been together for forty-five years? I can't imagine doing anything that long." Paul swatted at him playfully and he added, "Except being married to you of course."

"I had no idea this was their anniversary. That's so amazing," Paige said. "Your parents are basically my relationship role models. Even when I was a kid, I always thought I'd love to find someone who fit me as well as your mom and dad fit each other."

"It's pretty impressive," he agreed, "not that it was always easy."

"Oh, of course not." Paige had heard plenty of their arguments as a kid, and knew more than she probably should about the things they'd been through. But still, they'd made it.

"I wish I would have realized," Paige said. "I would have brought a gift."

"You know what Mom would say."

"Just having you here is the true gift," they both said in unison and laughed.

"It worked out so well that their anniversary was just after Ria retired too. She could finally be here instead of traveling all over the place, kicking that ball into a net."

"Wait. Retiring? Really?" Paige couldn't help but feel shocked. She couldn't picture Ria without a soccer ball at her feet. It had been that way since they tried out for their first team together when they were nine.

"Can you believe it?" Ria's voice broke in from behind her. "Hanging up the old cleats after all this time. Next World Cup I'll be watching from the sidelines like everyone else."

Paige watched her face, trying to gauge if this was a good thing or not. "I really can't believe it. What will you do with yourself?" She felt like she needed to sit down.

"Oh, I'm looking into some opportunities. But don't leak it to *Sports Illustrated* just yet. For now, I'm trying to learn how to relax." Ria laughed, but there was something behind it.

"Relax? You?" Paige deadpanned. "That's…new."

Ria stuck her tongue out in response as her younger brother, Benji, wandered up to join the group.

"It looks like I'm in the winner's circle," he joked, tucking a long strand of hair behind one ear. "Or maybe just the setup for a good joke: a conductor, a soccer player, and an artist walk into a bar."

"Well if it isn't the black sheep of the family," Ria said, swatting at him.

"Literal sheep," Jerald said. "Or haven't you heard, Paige? Our little brother is a farmer now."

"Really? Farming? Do tell, Benji." Paige knew he'd struggled over the years. She remembered when Mila had called Ria when they were still in the dorms to tell her that Benji had crashed the family car while drunk with his friends. He'd had to leave high school for rehab. He looked happy and healthy now, though, and she was so happy to see it.

"I am *so* glad that you asked," Benji said with a crooked grin. "Let me tell you about the joys of organic farming."

Everyone except Paige groaned audibly. Clearly, they had heard where this was going before.

"Where is your farm?" she asked. "Is it nearby?"

"It's in Paoli, just south of Bloomington. It's beautiful. I'm living on the farm and learning so much about planting crops and raising llamas and alpacas to make yarn. You should come down and see it sometime. I'd love to show you around."

"Will you make her shovel goat crap like you did when I visited?" Ria joked. "Can you believe it? I travel halfway around the world to see him, and I'm moving poop from one place to another. He sure knows how to show a girl a good time."

"Hey now," Paige said. "Unlike *some* people, I'm not afraid to get my hands dirty."

"Ooh," Jerald said. "She's got you there, Ria."

Paige felt herself easily sliding back into her old place, as though she'd never left. It was almost like nothing had ever happened.

But it did. The memory lodged in her chest like a stone. There was a reason she hadn't been here since college.

"Please excuse me for a minute," Paige said. She needed to breathe. "Can I get anyone a drink while I'm up?"

"Red wine, if you don't mind," Jerald said. Then with a glance from his husband, "Two actually, if you have enough hands."

"Not a problem," Paige promised.

She made her way up to the deck and through the sliding glass doors to the kitchen. Once inside, she felt a little calmer. She was the only one in the house at the moment, and it finally gave her a chance to clear her head. As much as she loved the Worths, they could be a little overwhelming.

She poured two glasses of wine for Jerald and Paul and popped open a beer for herself, but she wasn't quite ready to go back out into the melee. Just two days ago, she'd have sworn she'd never see the inside of this house again. But now that she was here, she couldn't resist the urge to look around and see if everything looked the same.

Leaving the drinks on the counter, she wandered into the living room. Mila had always loved home decorating and it showed. The house served as her office and she loved to entertain. The walls held evidence of the Worth kids' achievements, proudly displayed. Photos from birth through awkward teenage years to weddings documented them all as they grew. Paige was in one, hugging Ria as they grinned at the camera before their first day back to school, Jansport backpacks slung across their shoulders, a few teeth missing from their smiles. That photo hung next to framed newspaper articles praising Jerald's conducting career, followed by a photo from Amelia's law school graduation, one with Vina and her smiling husband and children, and of course, the ubiquitous photo of Ria and her team celebrating after they won the last World Cup.

She felt her chest tighten at the sight and grimaced. In another world, she would have celebrated that victory in the stands next to Ria's family. She would have been there to get a sweaty hug once the press was done begging for quotes and photos. But instead, she'd watched it alone in a sports bar in Broad Ripple, listening to the locals cheer as the team racked up goal after goal. She'd felt it then, and she felt it now, the hole in her chest that had been there for years. She couldn't help but wonder, would that hole ever heal?

The door to the lower level was open, and she couldn't resist taking a peek. She crept down the carpeted steps. Was it still there—her favorite place? She peeked under the stairs and there it was, as though she'd just left it a few minutes ago. Their hidden nook.

When they were kids, Paige and Ria would spend hours in their little hideaway. They'd even convinced Ria's dad to put up a curtain so they could be fully enclosed. They decorated the slanted ceiling with glow-in-the-dark star stickers and deemed it their own private clubhouse. Paige spent hours reading or drawing while Ria played her Game Boy or listened to Kris Kross on her new Discman. Sometimes they would just talk about all the things they were going to do when they were grown. All the countries they were going to visit. Who they were going to be and the adventures they were going to have.

Paige looked behind her, but no one seemed to be following. She crawled into the nook and pulled the curtain shut behind her. It was just the same. The stars still held a dim glow even after all these years. She leaned back and closed her eyes, drinking in the familiarity.

She wasn't sure how long it had been, but at some point she heard muffled footsteps. She hoped they would pass her by unnoticed, and for a moment, she thought they had. Then she heard a voice from the other side of the curtain.

"Paige, is that you?"

She knew that voice. She would know it anywhere. If she heard it on the other side of the world, or on another planet, she would know it was Ria. For a moment, she considered ignoring her, hoping she would go away and leave her in peace. But that wasn't fair. This was Ria's house, after all.

Paige tugged the curtain open. "I was just reminiscing," she said with a quiet smile.

"I don't blame you. Some kids have treehouses or forts built out of cardboard. We had this place."

"Yeah. It feels so strange that it was so long ago."

Ria hesitated, as though she was nervous. But Paige knew Ria was never nervous.

"Do you mind if I join you?"

Paige scooted over and patted the seat beside her. "Hop on in."

CHAPTER THREE

They sat quietly for a while, the air full of unspoken words. Paige had thought so many times over the years about what she would say to Ria if she ever saw her again, but now none of them seemed right. She opened her mouth and closed it several times, glad for the buffer of the semi-darkness around them.

Ria cleared her throat. "I'm glad you came tonight, Paige. I've really missed you."

Paige wanted to say *I missed you too. But I'm still so mad at you. Why did you do it? And why did you never say you were sorry?* But she didn't.

"It was sweet of your dad to invite me. You know how much I love your family."

"They ask about you all the time."

"So," she said, changing the subject, "how has it been? Playing soccer all over the world? Being on magazine covers and talk shows? Was it everything we used to imagine when we sat here telling ourselves how it would be?"

"It's been different, of course. But still good. I've been incredibly lucky, and I know it."

"I'm so glad for you, Ria. I really am. I always believed in you."

"I know. Honestly though? I'm tired of talking about myself. Let's talk about you. You've done well for yourself. I've seen some of the concert posters you've done. The first time I saw one, I was walking down a street in Berlin. We were there for a match. There must have been about thirty posters, all plastered up together on one wall. I stopped short and nearly collided with the guy in front of me because I knew, absolutely, that it was yours."

"How could you be so sure?"

"Your style is just so completely your own. Those almost doll-like people and animals you've been creating and evolving since we were kids. The way you can somehow show innocence and pain and happiness and every single other emotion through their big eyes. It may as well have had your signature on it."

"Wow. Thank you, Ria. That means a lot to me."

"I took a picture of it and I was going to text it to you, but then I remembered that we weren't talking anymore. I almost sent it anyway, but I was afraid of what you would text back. Or that you wouldn't text back at all."

"Oh." She didn't know what to say. She didn't know what she would have done back then if a text from Ria had shown up on her phone out of nowhere.

"I'm so proud of you, Paige. I really am. I mean, I've known you were awesome since we met in third grade, but I'm glad the rest of the world knows it now too."

Paige remembered the day they met, in the cafeteria, her first day in her new school. She'd had her lunch tray in her hands and was so scared to sit down with kids she didn't know. She'd felt paralyzed, wanted to run and hide. Ria had seen her standing there and invited her over to her table. Like it was no big deal. She'd asked her to come over and play after school too. And they'd been best friends ever after.

"I'm proud of you too, Ria. I guess we've both done all right for ourselves."

"The one regret I have," Ria said, turning to look at Paige, "is that I wasn't around to be there with you."

Paige felt like she could barely breathe, let alone speak.

"Do you think that maybe, just possibly, we could start over? Try to be friends again? I know it's a lot to ask, but I'd hate myself if I didn't try."

Tears formed in Paige's eyes, and one escaped and rolled down her face. She hoped the darkness hid its track. She had thought that what was broken couldn't be fixed, but now she wondered if maybe it could after all. Maybe they could seal up that one moment in time, the thing that split up their before and after, and bury it, grow something new on top of its grave. Be friends again. Forget they'd ever tried to be anything else. It was her best friend that she missed the most, and if she could have her back…

"I think I'd like that," Paige said. "I really would."

CHAPTER FOUR

Paige closed her eyes, listening to the album for which she was going to create the cover art. Her headphones blocked out all other sounds and let the music wash over her. The guys had added a banjo player this time, an interesting choice that seemed to work, even if it wasn't exactly her cup of tea. She tried to visualize a way to represent the feeling it gave her, as voices rose in harmony over the swelling strings. Creating specifically for someone else was such a different beast than making art for its own sake. Sometimes she started with color, and she was feeling an orange glow begin to emerge. Then the finger picking of the banjo suggested clouds to her, and a ladder leading from the ground below up into the firmament.

When she'd been in school, during her moments of deepest pretension, she might have turned up her nose at the idea of one of her pieces being on something as commercial as an album cover, or a concert poster, with words superimposed on top of the image she'd created. Or maybe not. Maybe she would have argued that art with function is still art, may even be more important art. At thirty-three years old, she now knew it wasn't possible to be a Puritan and still pay the bills. And she loved the posters she created, though she never could have predicted having this career. When The Slurs asked her to paint something for their first album, she thought it was just a fun side project, a favor for a friend with a band nobody had ever heard of. They had more of a psychedelic sound back then and she'd leaned into it, painting approximations of the band members with elongated proportions, being pulled into a black hole inside of a guitar. She'd been really proud of the piece, but didn't think anyone would really see it. And then they blew up. She started doing all their album covers and concert posters and somehow fans of the band also became fans of hers. Now people all around the world saw her art. Even better, they wanted to buy the prints she'd started selling through Etsy. The posters, the prints, and the occasional commission from people who wanted her to create something especially for them made it possible for her to live in Indianapolis as an artist and not have to work three jobs. It wasn't so easy for most of her friends, and she was grateful.

Unable to focus, she grabbed her phone to check her email, even though she knew once she picked up the phone that she'd get sucked in and lose an hour of productivity. She refreshed the screen and starting wading through her inbox, deleting the junk, flagging emails to come back to later. One email in particular stopped her short. It was from the Chicago Arts Commission.

She knew what this was. She'd been waiting for it, the results of the mural project she'd applied to. It was a long shot. The artist they chose would get to paint a huge mural in Boystown, the so-called gay-borhood of Chicago. Why was she so nervous to open this email? She knew it was probably one of those "thank you for applying but..." messages she was so used to. Even with all her success, some people still considered her work to be more illustration than art, though the lines finally seemed to be blurring. Artists like Tara MacPherson and Mark Ryden had carved out solid reputations in the realm of pop surrealism, a style influenced by cartoons and punk rock imagery. Not that she considered herself anywhere near their level.

Paige hovered her index finger over the email and pressed it, preparing herself for the inevitable rejection. *Just open it already, and then you can get back to work.*

The first few words made her gasp. "Congratulations! You have been selected..." The rest of it was a blur. She couldn't believe it. They'd actually picked her. Tens of thousands of people would see her work adorning the side of a city building for years. And an added bonus: the job paid well.

The project's manager, a Chicago gallery owner named Cara Bless Williams, asked her to come up to Chicago soon so they could visit the project site and discuss the details.

Paige let out a shriek of excitement and hoped her neighbors in the adjoining studios didn't hear her and think she was being murdered. With adrenaline flowing through her fingers, she wrote back, confirming that yes, she looked forward to meeting Ms. Williams and beginning work on the piece. Then, knowing she wouldn't be able to concentrate at all for the rest of the day, she texted Brandon. *Whatever you're doing, drop it. We're going out to celebrate, and the drinks are on me.*

She immediately saw the three wavering dots that meant he was typing back. *Lockerbie. 15 minutes. I look forward to destroying your tab.*

He wasn't kidding. When she arrived twenty minutes later, Brandon was already seated in one of the ancient-looking booths, holding a glass of some sort of dark liquid.

"You're late," he said. "I started without you. Don't forget to give the man your card."

"Big day?" the bartender asked her as she handed over her plastic. "Your friend over there told me to prepare for unwelcome outbursts of Irish song, and in about forty-five minutes a large order of assorted fried foods."

She laughed. "Something like that. Some good news, at least." She ordered another glass of whatever Brandon was drinking and an IPA for herself.

As she set the drinks on the table and climbed into the booth, Brandon looked at her expectantly.

"So, good news. Tell."

"I heard back about that project. The one in Chicago."

"And?"

"And they picked me! So basically, I'm going to be very big and important and I'll be moving immediately into my all-glass modern home where I'll make the furniture out of bubbles and cling wrap."

"As you should," he said, "though you will probably have to change your name now to something a little more unusual than Paige. At least a different spelling to show how truly creative you are. Perhaps Payje, with a 'y' and a 'j' in the middle. Or some sort of symbol, like Prince when he wanted to get out of his record contract. How were we supposed to pronounce that anyway?"

"It's the sound of one hand clapping, I'm pretty sure," she said, stone-faced.

Brandon reached over and pretended to clap her in the face with one hand and Paige pretended to be offended.

"Now, now, don't slap a gift horse in the mouth." She sat back in the booth, pulling her feet onto the cushioned bench. "So in other news, I think Ria and I are going to try and be friends."

Brandon raised one eyebrow. "Really, you don't say. Shall I issue the press release? This is news the world should know."

"It'll just get lost in the Friday news dump, I'm afraid. We'll have to wait for the tabloids to pick it up later."

"Speaking of those who want to know, does this mean I'll finally meet the infamous Ria?"

"Maybe." She bit her lip. "I'm not sure if we're hanging out friends at this point or just Christmas card friends."

He reached over as though he was going to hold her hand across the table. She looked at him skeptically. Before she could react, he snatched her phone off the table and typed in her code.

"You really need to use something other than our apartment number to protect this thing. Anyone could get in it," he said, already scrolling through her contacts. "Ah!" he said. "There's Ria. You've already put her number in here. You work fast."

"Give it back," she said, a little less amused. "And I've had her number since high school." Paige couldn't see what he was doing, but his fingers flew across the screen, which meant he was up to no good. "All right, you're hilarious. Give me my phone back." The phone dinged.

"Interesting," he said.

"What did you do?" she demanded. "I will punch you right in your trachea."

He grinned. "She'll be here in half an hour."

Twenty minutes later, Paige watched the door apprehensively. "So when did you decide you want to die today?" she asked Brandon.

"I want to meet her." He smiled sweetly. "After all, how often does a guy get to meet a real live WNBA star?"

"You're hilarious. You know she plays soccer."

"Don't you mean football? Or rather, *fútbol*," he said in a terrible fake accent. "Excuse me, I think my drink needs freshening." He got up and headed for the bar.

"That expression makes no sense," she called after him. "You're not making your drink fresher, you're getting a new one."

He turned and smiled over his shoulder and then stepped up to the bar and immediately became involved in an animated discussion with the bartender. Paige sighed. When she'd said she wanted to be friends with Ria, she meant the kind of friends who say hello if they ran into each other somewhere unexpectedly, not the kind who made plans on purpose. At least not yet.

It was hard to believe they had once seen each other every single day and talked on the phone for hours in between. Now they were nearly strangers. But that's not so unusual for childhood friendships, she thought. Sometimes they're so intense, but then we outgrow them, leave them behind in yearbooks and memories. She couldn't help but wonder if that's what would have happened to them, if there would have been a slow fade into Facebook likes and *Oh yeah, we should catch up soon* messages, if everything else hadn't happened. But she was letting that go now. It was time.

When Ria walked in, Paige's heart leapt in her chest. She really needed it to stop doing that. Ria just had that effect on people. All through high school and college, girls had thrown themselves at her. Guys too. She could have had anyone she wanted, and she often did. Paige would tease her about always dating the straight girls. While Paige had a couple longer relationships with girls Ria considered much too butch, Ria spent her time with the cheerleaders and homecoming queens. The bigger the challenge, the more she wanted them.

"How do you do it?" Paige had once asked, after Ria confessed she'd been spending time with Missy Walkens, the quarterback's girlfriend.

"I don't know," Ria had replied with a sly grin. "But can you blame her? I'm much cuter than Grant Hughes. And I have much less body hair."

"Well thank god for that," Paige said.

But it was true that Ria had the charm that came naturally to politicians and actors. Paige wished she had it, but she just couldn't figure out how to have that kind of charisma. It seemed like something in Ria's bones and breath, the way she moved and spoke, that made everyone love her and want to be loved by her.

Sometimes Paige had wondered why Ria chose her as a best friend, when she could have had anyone. But then Paige reminded herself that she was pretty badass in her own right. People may have noticed Ria more than Paige, but Paige had done all right for herself in the end.

CHAPTER FIVE

Ria squinted into the bar's dim light, so much darker than the summer daylight outside. She took off her Ray Bans and hung them on the V of her t-shirt as she scanned the bar.

Paige waived and when Ria saw her, she smiled and headed her way.

"Hey lady," Paige whispered as she sat down. "I don't know if you noticed, but I think people are staring at you."

Ria looked around the mostly empty bar. There were only a few patrons but they did seem to be looking their way.

"You mean those four people? I better be careful, one of them might be TMZ."

"You laugh," Paige said, "but I don't think you realize how obsessed Indy was with you during the last World Cup. You were right up there with David Letterman for best-loved homegrown celebrity."

Ria laughed. "Well, it's not like I have a lot of competition."

"Hey now, we've got James Dean, and part of Abraham Lincoln's childhood. That's pretty impressive company. But seriously, I wish you could have seen the watch parties here during your matches. It was insane."

"Does that mean you were watching?"

Paige's face colored. "I mean, yeah, of course. Like I could miss that."

Ria grinned. "I'm glad you invited me out today. I haven't had a chance to relax since I got home, and now we can really catch up."

"Well technically, Brandon invited you from my phone."

Ria's face fell. "Oh."

"But I'm glad you're here," Paige reassured her.

"So who's Brandon?"

"My roommate. He's over there, trying to drink my bank account dry." Brandon waved from the bar.

"That's a big dude. Good luck with that bar tab. Are you buying everyone's drinks today? Because I have several dry months of training to make up for." Ria winked at her.

"So how has it been? The retirement."

"Shh… remember, not public knowledge yet."

"Right. Can't tip off the paparazzi. They're everywhere around here."

Ria leaned back into the booth so that her back was against the wall, her legs outstretched along the bench's length. Paige couldn't help but notice that she favored her left knee. She remembered when Ria messed it up in college, and Paige wondered if it was still giving her trouble.

"I don't think it's really hit me yet. After the Cup, we played a victory tour in a bunch of cities and did a lot of appearances and press. Did you know I got to meet Obama? Now *that* was a president."

"That's amazing."

"He's even better in person—funny, and not too bad to look at. It was pretty surreal. After that, I went back to my team in Seattle and played for the National League for a little while, but I guess I knew I was winding down. And now I've been…well… Can you keep a secret?"

"Of course. I never did tell anyone where we buried that time capsule."

"Oh god, I forgot all about that. It's probably still under the backyard."

"Probably pretty gross and moldy by now."

"Ew. Anyhow, I've been taking interviews for coaching gigs."

Paige laughed. "No way. You, a coach?"

Ria affected a wounded look. "You don't think I could coach?"

"Oh, no. You'd be a great coach, I'm sure. I guess I've just never imagined you not being one with the ball."

"Me neither, at least until the past couple years. One of the things they don't tell you when you start playing sports is how beat up your body is going to get, especially when you get older."

"You're only thirty-three."

"Yeah, but athletes age in dog years. So I'm really a hundred and fifty."

"You look pretty good for being a century and a half."

Brandon strode up to the table and coughed to get their attention, his hands full of glasses.

"When I told you I'd get the tab, I didn't mean you should drink all of the alcohol in the entire bar at once." Paige deadpanned.

"You said we were celebrating," he retorted. "I'm just much, much better at celebrating than you are. Anyhow, one of these drinks is for our esteemed guest. I wasn't sure what you wanted, so I got you options—Sun King Osiris like our friend Paige here, or the classic Johnny Walker Black on the rocks, like me. No pressure, but I will absolutely judge you on the choice you make."

"Well in that case…" Ria reached with both hands and took one of each, immediately downing the whiskey and handing the empty glass back to him. Brandon nodded his approval.

"You know," Ria said, "My mother told me never to accept drinks from strange men."

"Strange? Me?" Brandon feigned offense. "I am your perfectly ordinary, run of the mill, Brandon. Pleased to make your acquaintance, by the way." He held out a hand and bent at the waist, as if greeting royalty.

Ria took his hand and nodded a mock curtsy. "I'm Ria, but I take it you already know that, since apparently you were the one who invited me to this little party. What's the occasion anyway? Paige has been remiss at filling me in."

"She didn't tell you? Typical. She's always keeping the good news to herself."

"She always has," Ria replied. Paige looked at her sideways. What was that supposed to mean?

"Well, go on, rock star," Brandon insisted. "Tell her what you've won."

Paige felt embarrassed. "I didn't win anything. I just got a job. A mural in Chicago."

"Oh, please," Brandon interrupted. "She got picked out of hundreds or thousands of artists to do a huge mural in Boystown. And they're paying her actual money instead of a year's supply of hot dogs, which is what I imagine they typically use for currency up in Chicago."

"Paige, that's amazing," Ria said. "Congratulations."

"It's all right."

"Don't do that. Don't underplay your achievements." She turned to Brandon. "She's always been this ridiculously talented. Did you know that? When we were little kids, she would draw everything she saw, from trees to soccer balls to dirty laundry."

"It was tough to really invoke the smell of the dirty laundry," Paige said, "but I think I did it justice."

Brandon made an exaggerated slurping sound and held up his glass, which now contained only a few melting ice cubes. "Down the hatch, as they say. Anyone for round two?"

"Round two?" Paige looked at him sternly. "I don't think you're using solid math skills here. And you should know, Ria is a certified mathematician and you can't get anything by her."

"Seriously?" Brandon looked impressed.

"I can add a little," Ria said, "but who's counting?" She gave Paige a look that meant trouble, raised her glass of beer, and drained it dry.

"Did Paige ever tell you about when we went to the World Cup back in '99?" Ria asked a few rounds later, her words slurring just a little.

"No! Was that the year that—"

"That Brandi Chastain tore off her shirt and ran around in her sports bra?"

"How'd you know what I was going to say?" Brandon laughed. "Am I that predictable?"

"You're a dude. But, I can't blame you. It was iconic. And, okay, yes, she was pretty damn hot."

"But Mia Hamm," Paige said, her voice dreamy. "She was the best."

"God, that team had so many great players. I always wanted to play like them. Every single person was so strong, and they fit together so well. You know, Paige, I always thought you were a little like Mia."

"Wait, wait, hold on," Brandon said. "Paige played soccer?"

"I told you that."

"Yeah, but not that you were, like, any good at it."

"I was never as good as Ria. And I quit in eighth grade."

"She could have been amazing, if she'd wanted it," Ria insisted. "She was a really good defensive player, and she could set you up beautifully for a shot. But her heart wasn't in it, you know? We always knew she was going to be our Georgia O'Keefe instead."

Paige tried to steer the conversation back on track. "So, the World Cup in 1999. We were sixteen, I think, and Ria was as soccer-crazed as ever. We'd been watching every game on TV, taping them and rewinding them over and over again to see how they pulled those crazy moves. They were playing in California at the Rose Bowl. We would yell at the TV like we were there in the stadium. The day before the final game, Ria's dad pulled us aside and said we needed to talk. It was terrifying."

"We were so sure he'd caught on that we were sneaking his vodka and replacing it with water," Ria giggled. "He said, 'Listen girls, I know you love soccer but you're getting a little out of hand.' We looked at each other, totally confused. He loved soccer too, and he loved that we loved it. And then he said,

'Your mom can't handle the noise anymore. So, the only thing we can do is…' And he held up plane tickets and said, 'Get on out to sunny California to see the last game in person!'"

"We were so excited we probably didn't stop screaming for ten minutes."

"He totally surprised us. I had no idea he was going to do that."

"Your dad has always been awesome. It's exactly the kind of thing he would do."

"Yeah, you're right."

"And was the game as amazing in person as it was on TV?" Brandon asked.

"Oh god, yes," Ria said fervently. "I can still see every last play in my mind. I screamed so loud that I lost my voice for a week."

"And don't forget, you made me paint my belly in red, white, and blue."

"Hey, you were the one who decided what we should paint."

"Ha. Oh yeah."

"What did you paint?" Brandon asked.

"Paige was so in love with Mia Hamm. I loved Mia too, but Carla Overbeck was my girl. So of course, I painted Mia on my stomach, and Paige painted Hamm."

"Do you think she saw you?"

"Oh, she saw us," Paige said. "Ria's dad doesn't do anything halfway. Our seats were so close that I swear we could smell the players' sweat."

"Sounds…fragrant."

"We were screaming U-S-A and 'Mia Hamm' over and over. I swear she looked up at us and winked."

"I was lucky Paige didn't pass out."

"Oh, like you were so cool." Paige made a face.

"Do you remember the game ended in a shootout? God, I thought I was going to barf I was so nervous. But they did it. Of course they did."

"I can't believe it was that close and we got to see it. I should thank your dad again for that sometime. It's probably one of my top ten memories."

"Oh, top five for sure."

"But little did we know that you were going to grow up to be just as good as any player on that team."

"You didn't?" Ria affected a wounded expression.

"Okay fine, we did, but it's not like we needed to make your ego any bigger."

"Ouch. I think my ego is perfectly sized for my head."

"True. You've always had an abnormally large head."

"Well, ladies," Brandon broke in. "I hate to interrupt this stroll down memory lane, but I have students tomorrow, and I need at least a solid five hours if I'm going to listen to off-key singing without murdering someone."

Paige and Ria looked outside and both seemed shocked that the sky was solidly black.

"Oh, crap," Ria said. "When did it get so dark?" She looked at her phone. "It's almost midnight!"

"Do you turn into a pumpkin at midnight?" Paige asked, not quite ready to go home.

"No, but I have a thing tomorrow." Ria pulled out her phone and ordered an Uber. "He'll be here in about ten minutes. Do you want a ride?"

"We're going the opposite way. What kind of thing do you have tomorrow?"

"Something at our old school."

"Oh, are you going to give a motivational speech or something? Tell kids to stay off the drugs and play sports instead?"

"Kind of. But I'll tell them that pot is okay, unless you're going to be drug tested within thirty days."

"Good advice," Brandon said. "Hey, I'll go settle up. Paige, you're giving the bartender a really good tip."

"Great."

"I should probably wait outside," Ria said.

"I'll wait with you."

The street was quiet, the evening air cool, only a few cars passing by. They waited in the soft glow of the street lamps.

"So you're really giving a speech at the school? Who would have imagined?"

Ria looked a little embarrassed. "Okay, fine, they're naming one of the gyms after me."

"Wait, there's more than one gym at the high school now? And your name is going to be on one? No way."

"Yep. I always dreamed about having my name on the smelliest part of the school."

"That's so great, Ria. You deserve it."

"Because I'm smelly?"

"Exactly."

Ria hesitated. "You know, you're welcome to come if you want. The family will all be there. Well, except for Jer, he had to head home. It'll probably be kinda lame, you know, all those kids being forced to come listen to me talk when they'd rather be making out with each other in the hallway. But it would be cool if you came. Like we came full circle. If you don't have to work, or, I mean, have other things you need to do. I know you have a life."

Paige wasn't sure if it was the drinks, or the night that felt like a dream, but she felt so glad to have Ria back in her life again. Ria smiled at her and she felt surrounded in warmth.

"Of course I'll go. I wouldn't miss it."

"Paige…" Ria said, stepping closer.

Paige looked into her eyes. What was she so worried about? She reached out and took Ria's hand and a feeling shot through her whole body. Ria bit her lip, as though she was unsure and pulled her closer. In the back of Paige's mind, a little voice told her to wait, that this might not be a great idea, but she told the voice to shut up.

A car rolled to a stop right next to them. They barely noticed, standing there, looking at each other, until a man coughed. "Someone call an Uber?"

It broke the spell. Paige flushed, embarrassed to be caught in such a private moment.

"That's me," Ria said. "Just a second," she told the driver.

"Guess you better go," Paige whispered.

"I guess so. But you'll be there tomorrow, right?"

"I'll be there."

Ria wrapped her in a tight hug and let her go. "Thanks for a great night. And congrats again on your mural project."

"Oh right, that. Thanks." She could barely corral her thoughts.

She watched as Ria climbed in the car and shut the door, waving as it pulled away. Once it was out of sight, Paige finally let the out the breath she was holding.

CHAPTER SIX

"What the hell?" Paige said to herself, once she'd finally woken up. That was not how she had expected her evening to go. What even was that?

She tore herself out of bed, her head reminding her that drinking in her thirties was much different than back in her college days. Though it seemed to have much the same effect on her behavior.

Brandon had already left for the day, but bless that man, he'd left half a pot of coffee behind. As the caffeine seeped into her brain, she couldn't help but obsess about it. Could she blame it on the beer and the shots? So much for being older and wiser. It wasn't even what she wanted, right? They'd just started talking again, after all. Why take the risk of blowing things up all over again? But still, she couldn't help that part of her that wondered what if.

Oh god, it was already late in the morning, and she'd promised to go to the gym dedication. Downing the rest of the coffee, Paige forced herself into the shower.

She had thought that her old high school would look smaller now that she was older. But if anything, it looked even bigger. The school had only grown in the years since she and Ria walked its halls. Even back then she'd thought there were too many kids for one school, but the district didn't want to add a second high school and dilute their sports teams' talent pools.

That made it all the more incredible that Ria had been such a superstar on the high school team. By her sophomore year, she already played more minutes each game than most of the seniors. If there was such a thing as fate, Ria was meant to be a soccer star. And it felt only right that they were back here again to recognize her for it.

Paige checked in at the front desk and showed her ID, explaining that she was there for Ria's ceremony as a friend of the family. After signing in, they gave her a visitor's badge. They didn't have this kind of security back in the day, she thought. Now cameras dotted the hallways and visitors were carefully scrutinized before they entered the building. She was glad she'd gone to school before all of this was necessary.

Finding herself swept up in a sea of students, she followed along as they headed toward the gymnasium where Ria would speak to the senior class and cut the ribbon dedicating the building as the Ria Worth Sports Gym. The kids looked so young that Paige couldn't tell if they looked younger now, or if she was just losing her ability to guess people's ages. Did she look old to them?

When she'd gone here, she couldn't have imagined what life would be like at thirty-three. The life ahead looked like one big blur, like a canvas she hadn't even begun to paint. Ria was probably the only person she'd known who had a true plan and the drive to follow through. Paige had her own passions, but unlike Ria's, they didn't lead her down a straight path.

The pack of teenage girls in front of her spoke loudly and somehow managed to walk, talk, and text on their phones all at the same time without tripping. That was some kind of talent. She couldn't help overhearing them.

"At first I thought this would be totally lame, but have you seen a picture of Ria? She's hot," a tall blonde in a short skirt said with a laugh.

"Oh totally," a shorter brunette answered. "I would definitely fence jump for her."

The group laughed and their conversation rolled on to different subjects. Paige laughed to herself and shook her head. Ria still had it. And it was amazing to hear the kids talking so openly. While they hadn't been secretive, she and Ria still hadn't talked about girls loudly in the hallways. Maybe everything had changed and kids didn't have to worry about that kind of thing anymore. Maybe they just worried about the million other things that set them apart and made them different. It made her smile and also made her feel like a dinosaur.

The students converged on the entrance to the gym. Paige looked up as she walked inside. The building had received a makeover since she was in it last, but state championship banners still hung in the rafters, declaring the Carmel High School Greyhounds winners. She searched around until she found Ria's IHSAA banners—two of them—her sophomore and senior years. They may as well have belonged to Ria. She was always the star and without her, they probably wouldn't have won.

Someone off to the side of the gym caught her eye and waved. Mila. Paige smiled and waved back, picking her way around the chattering teens to meet her.

"This is amazing," she said when she finally reached Mila and the rest of the family. "I feel like I've gone back in time a little."

"Like Doctor Who!" Mila said with a laugh.

"You watch Doctor Who, Mila?"

"Oh yes, but I do miss David Tennant. He was my favorite Doctor."

"We'll have to debate that later. I'm still soft on Christopher Eccleston, even though he just had that one season."

The loudspeaker made a high-pitched squeal, and everyone winced and covered their ears. *Well, some things never change.*

"Please make your way to your seats," the disembodied voice insisted. "Our program is about to begin."

"This is so cool," Benji said, shouldering his way through the crowd. "Who would have thought when we were kids that we'd be back here for something like this?"

"I would have," Henry replied.

It was true. Henry had always believed Ria could do anything, and he somehow managed to avoid being the cliché type of soccer dad. He cheered and supported, but he didn't scream and berate the coaches and try to run the games himself from the sidelines like so many other parents. That was probably a big reason why Ria never burned out. Paige had seen the constant commentary and the pressure from the other parents. She'd seen the light in the other kids' eyes go slowly out as their love of the game was replaced by the trepidation of disappointing their moms or dads. Ria was damn lucky.

The Worth family was still the same—still proud of Ria, still cheering and showing up anywhere they could to show support for her. Paige felt lucky to have found this family. Once they'd decided she was part of it, they'd given her all the same support.

That never took away from her own dad. Even though he'd been working a lot when she was a kid, she knew he'd been doing it for her. It couldn't have been easy for him, and she loved him all the more for it.

The crowd quieted as Ria made her way to the center of the gym floor, flanked by administrators and a few teachers. Paige didn't recognize any of them. Surely some of her former teachers were still there. It had only been fifteen years, but if they were there, she didn't see them.

A tall, partially bald man in a suit strolled up to the mic and coughed into it to get everyone's attention. Paige figured he must be the principal.

"Thank you, everyone, for joining us this afternoon for this honorable occasion. I'm sure you all have heard of our hometown hero and today's guest of honor, Ria Worth, but please allow me a few minutes to share some key features of her biography.

"Ria graduated in our class of 2001, and even then we knew she was talented and destined for greatness. She is a shining example of what Carmel High School's athletes can achieve when paired with dedication, passion, and grit. She was a key member of our girls' soccer team for all four years of her high school career, scoring many goals along the way, and twice leading the team to state victory. In the year 2000, she received the title of Indiana Girls' Soccer Athlete of the Year, and she has not slowed down since.

"After graduating from these hallowed halls, Ria accepted a scholarship to Indiana University, where she quickly became an MVP of their girls' team. Her scholarship, like many of the sports-based scholarships our students have received over the years, demonstrates the important intersection of athletics and academics."

Benji chuckled a little under his breath, and Paige exchanged grins with him. She knew what he was thinking. Academics had been the least of Ria's worries. The girl was naturally smart and her teachers loved her, but soccer was her first and only true love. School was a chore to get through on the way to the field. Paige had always been a little jealous that schools seemed to value sports above all else—including art—but she was never jealous of Ria.

The principal continued narrating Ria's path toward the Olympics and the World Cup. He missed plenty of details, but the broad strokes were all true. Finally he concluded.

"We are so proud to have Ria Worth back on our campus today to dedicate this gym. But before we get to the official ribbon-cutting, she would like to say a few words." He moved aside as Ria stepped up to the mic.

She pulled it off the stand and looked around the room, taking it all in. Then she smiled.

"You guys, this is pretty amazing. Well, at least for me. You're probably just glad to have an excuse to skip class." The kids laughed.

"I don't blame you. I was an okay student but I lived for soccer. Sorry, Principal Daniels, but it's true. I would get so annoyed at having to learn all these things I didn't think I'd need in the real world. But a weird thing happened along the way. All those random things I had to learn? A lot of them came in handy. And not just at trivia night at the bar.

"About halfway through college I realized something. That it wasn't just about memorizing facts and calculations and historical events. Learning those things was a kind of training, just like the drills at soccer practice. They were teaching me how to think. How to solve problems. How to evaluate information. And a weird thing happened that I never could have imagined—I fell in love with math." Assorted groans echoed throughout the gym.

"I know!" Ria grinned. "It sounds insane, right? Everyone hates math. I hated math! Or so I thought. But my freshman year of college, I took the required math class, Finite Mathematics, or something else complicated like that. I was hoping to skate by on a 'C' since that was the lowest grade you could get and still have the class count and not have your coach yell at you.

"And probably that's what I would have done, except that I had an amazing professor. She was actually an adjunct professor, which is slang for teaching a class like a regular professor but getting paid crap. She taught math like it was interesting, like it was something she was excited to be teaching. And that enthusiasm worked. It made me interested. All of a sudden, it wasn't a chore to learn how the numbers fit together. It was a puzzle. It was like watching the game play out on the field, seeing where the players were located, what direction they were going and how fast, all of those things my brain just naturally figured out.

"I decided to major in math, which I know might sound crazy. But it spoke to me. And I really think it made me a better player too. I could bring more to the team. So don't let anyone tell you all jocks are dumb. Yeah, if you interview us right after a game, we're going to sound like idiots because our blood is everywhere in our bodies except our brains, but some of the smartest people I've met are athletes.

"School is a tool. Use it. Take every kind of class, because you never know what you're going to love. And enjoy it. Because once you graduate, you don't get summer break anymore, and that's really unfortunate. Thank you." She handed the microphone back to the principal as the student body clapped.

"Everyone please join us at the entrance to the gym for the symbolic ribbon cutting of the building that will now bear Ria's name." And with that, they were dismissed. The Worths hustled to beat the crowd. Even now, Ria's parents photographed every milestone. Paige tagged along.

"That was awesome," Benji said. "Did you see how she had those kids just eating out of the palm of her hand?"

"I know, they actually seemed interested in what she was saying. That's no small thing." Paige was starting to see how Ria might be a good coach. If she could hold these kids' attention, just imagine the impact she could have on college students.

"Do you want to go out for lunch with us after this, Paige?" Mila asked.

"Sure, Mila, that would be nice. Thanks for the invitation."

It was funny how easy it was to slip back into this family. It was as though all those years she'd been away never happened, like they'd been erased. They'd barely given her a hard time about it. Maybe they were just as glad as she was that things were back to normal.

Ria and the VIPs posed outside by the entrance, as a crowd of students gathered in front of them, a few of them busily Instagramming the moment and each other. Ria's mom had her camera ready and was trying to get Ria's attention. Ria scanned the crowd and smiled when she found them. She waved a hand. Paige raised a hand to wave back, but Ria's expression changed to something like surprise and a pleasant confusion.

Paige turned around and saw a woman waving her fingers at Ria, smiling broadly. Tall and willowy, her effortlessly tousled, shiny brown locks tumbled down her back. The woman carried a small suitcase, the kind of luggage that Paige knew cost more than her monthly rent. Benji turned to see what caught Paige's attention.

"Oh hey," he said. "Elena's here. I didn't know she was coming."

Elena. Paige's stomach dropped. She already knew who that was, though she'd never seen her in person. Ria had mentioned her in interviews, being thankful for, "the support of my wonderful partner, Elena Martine." Gossip sites had posted photos of them leaving various restaurants together, their fingers intertwined as they walked. But they had split up a couple years ago, hadn't they? Or maybe not. Elena was from Europe—Spain, Paige thought she remembered reading—so what was she doing here now?

"Here we go!" Mila said, holding up her phone to record the moment for posterity.

Holding an oversized pair of scissors, Ria held them open over the red ribbon tied across the gym doors and smiled for the cameras before she cut it free.

CHAPTER SEVEN

The family descended upon an unsuspecting restaurant not far from the high school, the kind of restaurant that offers small plates of food that are somehow also supposed to be shared. The waiter looked a little panicked when they asked for a table for nine outside, but it wasn't particularly busy. After a few minutes of completely rearranging the furniture, he led them to the tables that had been shoved together to accommodate them.

"Elena, come sit by me!" Mila called out. Paige fought off a pang of jealousy. She hadn't known that Elena was so close to the family. And god, did she have to be so pretty? Ria had always dated girls who looked like models. She felt her usual confidence dissipate.

Paige found herself sitting next to Vina and her four year old, Kelsey. The toddler excitedly told her all about the field trip they'd taken to the Children's Museum last week. She tried to pay attention and look excited, but she strained to hear snippets of the conversation between Ria, Elena, Mila, and Henry at the other side of the table. She made eye contact with Ria a couple times, and she smiled and acted as though she was having a great time even though she didn't feel it. She'd started feeling like she was a part of the family again, but just like that, she realized how far away they were.

They ordered half the items on the menu and passed them from person to person until everyone was well and truly full.

What am I doing here? Paige shifted awkwardly in her seat. She surreptitiously checked the time on her phone, trying to think of an excuse to go that wouldn't be obvious. Not wanting to be rude, she tried to listen to Benji's stories about the farm and what Kelsey was learning in preschool, silently begging for the meal to be over so she could escape.

Ria, her parents, and Elena were all smiling and making excited gestures. Elena laid her hand on Ria's wrist and whispered something into her ear, and Paige felt the bottom fall out. It was like looking through a window into a place she no longer fit in.

Finally all the plates were empty, the leftovers boxed up to send home to Vina's always-hungry brood, and the check paid. All of the siblings insisted they were going to pay, but Ria's dad shot them down.

"How often do I have you all here together? And we got to visit Ria's high school without it being because she got in trouble! I am more than happy to pick up the check for an occasion like this."

"Is everyone coming back to the house?" Mila asked the group. "I have a cake and we have that espresso maker we never use."

"Sorry mom," Vina said, helping Kelsey gather up her things. "We have to run a couple errands before the other kids get home from school."

Paige took that as her cue and got up to leave as well.

"Oh Paige! Not you too! You must come back with us."

"I really wish that I could," she fibbed, "but I have a big project I have to get working on."

"Yes! Ria told us about your wonderful large painting in Chicago. How exciting!"

"Thank you so much. And thank you for lunch. It was very sweet of you to invite me."

Paige mumbled her goodbyes to everyone and walked quickly out of the restaurant. Halfway to her car, Ria caught up with her.

"Paige! Hold up!"

"Oh hey, Ria." Paige fumbled with her keys. "Congrats again on today. That was very cool. Thank you for inviting me."

"I just wanted to say I'm sorry we didn't get to talk much. I had no idea Elena was coming. She's unpredictable like that."

"It's not a problem. Hey, I need to go."

"Hold on. I had a good time hanging out with you last night. We should do it again sometime."

"Yeah. That would be nice. You should bring Elena."

"Oh. Maybe, I guess. I don't really know what her plans are."

"That's cool. Anyway, I've got to go. I'll talk to you soon."

Paige turned and rushed off to her car, afraid to say anything else. *God I'm such an idiot.* How had she managed to get her head turned around again so easily? Maybe they could be friends, but that was going to be it. She was going to focus on work. That was what was really important right now.

Instead of heading to her studio, Paige drove out to Garfield Park, her favorite place in the city to be alone with her thoughts, a pencil, and a blank pad of paper. She knew she should be working on refining her design for the mural, but when she felt like this, it was best to just start drawing without a goal in mind.

The park was quiet today. The kids weren't out of school just yet, and the pack of guys who sometimes lurked around must have either been on the other side of the park, or they'd gone off to score some food or drugs. Either way, she had the Sunken Gardens to herself. Somehow she'd managed to go through her entire childhood without ever visiting this park, and she'd only discovered it once she moved back, even though it was over a hundred years old.

It was a huge park, with different pockets—tennis courts, a pagoda, jungle gyms, and lots of green grass, but the Sunken

Gardens were her favorite part. The ancient fountain shot water skyward in calming arcs in the center of the formal garden. Depending on the season, the park planted different types of flowers, and Paige loved it best when the tulips bloomed. They were past that now. The summer plants were already blossoming.

She found a stone bench and sat cross-legged on it, pulled her pencils and notebook out of her messenger bag. Maybe she could clear her head by sketching some flowers. She tried outlining some of the newly planted annuals, but she couldn't concentrate. How had she let this happen again? How had she let herself get all mixed up when she knew better? It wasn't as bad as before, thank god for that. She'd been so stupid. It might as well have been yesterday for how little time had eroded the memory.

If she had a time machine, she'd travel back to the end of senior year at IU and tell herself not to answer the door that night. That night when she'd fallen asleep on the couch studying for finals and woken up to someone knocking loudly.

She'd glanced at the clock. It was midnight, a little too early for a college student to be asleep on a Friday, but senior year was so much different than when she was a freshman and wanted to go out to parties all night. She was just now hearing back from the grad schools she'd applied to, with one exciting prospect having come in just that day. Grades didn't really matter at that point, now that her applications were all out, but it still mattered to her. She cracked her back and uncurled herself from the couch cushions. The knocking continued, its volume only increasing.

"Paige!" Ria's voice called out from behind the door. "Your light's on. Are you in there?"

"Jesus, Ria," she mumbled as she undid the chain and pulled the door open. "Dude. You're going to get me reported to the leasing office."

Ria smiled big, and Paige realized that Ria was completely and utterly drunk.

"You better come inside." She led Ria to the couch and went straight to her tiny kitchenette to make coffee.

"Please tell me you didn't drive," she called out behind her as Ria made herself at home.

"Nope. I got a ride. I'm in no condition to be operating a motor vehicle at this juncture."

She laughed. Ria was the one person she knew whose vocabulary actually increased when she'd been drinking.

"All right, well at least you were safe. But why, exactly, are you showing up at my apartment in the middle of the night, drunk off your head?"

"That is a very good question." Ria smiled. "I want to tell you my good news!"

"You have news at midnight?"

"Well, I had news at six o'clock, but then I fell into a pitcher of Hairy Bears."

"Yikes," she replied. "I haven't had one of those in a couple years now. They're pretty lethal."

"They are very potent and also cost-effective."

Paige sat next to Ria on the couch and turned toward her. "So what's this news? Don't leave me in suspense."

Ria looked up at Paige, her face bright. "I got the call."

"The call?"

"*The* call. The coach of the women's national team called me."

"Oh my god. What did he say?"

"He said that…" She hiccupped. "Well, he said that I'm still not ready yet."

"Hold on. That doesn't exactly sound like good news."

"But wait! There's more."

"Okay…"

"He wants me to go play for a year in Europe, and then he wants me to come back for camp. He said if I can improve my teamwork that I might have a shot after all."

"Ria, that's awesome!"

"Right? He already talked to a team in France and they want me to come play after graduation."

"You're going to France? That's amazing!"

"I'm going to eat all of the cheese and drink all of the wine."

"And then roll down the soccer field," Paige joked.

"Yes, I will become the ball. Completely round. And I will squash all other teams when they attempt to score on me. I'll roll right over their feet."

"Well now I see why you went out and got wasted. That is definitely worth celebrating."

"Speaking of drunk, I think we should toast," Ria said.

"I think if you have any more to drink you might barf all over my sofa."

"Fine. I'll have some of that coffee, and you have some sort of booze, and we'll toast with that."

"Fair enough." She poured Ria a cup of the freshly brewed coffee and grabbed a beer from the fridge.

They held their drinks up.

"To being the ball," Paige said.

"To getting what we've always wanted."

They clinked their drinks and took a sip.

"Ow. Hot." Ria stuck out her burned tongue. Paige laughed and rolled her eyes.

Ria set her coffee mug on a side table and turned back to Paige. She got a funny look in her eyes.

"What?" Paige asked.

Ria looked at her and bit her lip, considering something. Then she leaned forward and pressed her lips against Paige's.

For a moment Paige fell into the kiss. She let the room dissolve around her. It felt like something she'd been waiting for. And then her eyes flew open, and she jerked back.

"Ria, what are you doing?"

"I'm kissing you."

"You're drunk."

"True. And that may be giving me the guts to kiss you, but it's not *why* I'm kissing you," Ria said firmly. "I'm kissing you because I've always wanted to, but I was afraid to do it."

Paige got up and started neatening the room.

"What are you doing?"

"You know when I get stressed or upset I clean. Well this… It makes me want to clean the whole house."

"Stop," Ria said. "Come back."

"No. Ria, I've seen you hook up with so many girls. I know you got awesome news today and you went out to celebrate, and you want to celebrate more, but I don't want to be one of your girls."

Ria got up from the couch and walked over to Paige. She seemed soberer with every step.

"Paige, please stop. Look at me."

She looked up, afraid that if she met Ria's eyes she would cry. Ria put her hands on Paige's arms and looked into her face.

"I love you."

Paige felt like she couldn't breathe, let alone speak.

"Ria, you're drunk. You don't know what you're saying."

"Yes I do. I think I've loved you ever since we met in the cafeteria in third grade. And every day since then. But we were such good friends that I was afraid if I reached for anything more I would ruin it. I'd rather have you as my friend than lose you. But I don't want to hide it anymore. I can't go live millions of miles away without letting you know. I love you so much, Paige. I love you."

Tears streamed down Paige's cheeks. She bit her lip and closed her eyes.

"I love you too," she whispered. Years of hidden emotions burst out of her chest. "I saw you date girl after girl, but you'd always move on and never see them again. I didn't want that. So I just told myself I was happy being your friend. I mostly believed it. But damn it, Ria, I love you too."

Paige pushed Ria against the wall. Ria leaned into her embrace, her body giving way just enough. She ran her fingers through the hair at the nape of Paige's neck and tugged. The temperature in the room seemed to rise. *Oh my god. This is really happening.*

She ran her hands under Ria's button-down shirt and the tank top underneath, feeling her skin warm beneath her fingers. They stared into each other's eyes and something new was there, something hidden that was finally released. It was as though the tension that had built for years could no longer be ignored. They both knew where this was going.

Paige led Ria past the kitchen, down the narrow hall and into her bedroom.

"I've never been in here before," Ria said, as Paige kicked the bedroom door shut behind them.

"Let me show you around then."

Paige cupped her hand against Ria's cheek and Ria bit her palm. "Fuck," she sighed.

"Yeah."

Pressed up against the post at the end of the bed, Ria kissed her neck and breathed against her ear. "God, Paige, I want you."

Paige reached under Ria's shirts and lifted them up and over her head. She gave her a slight push and they collapsed on the mattress. She sat up, looking down at Ria, taking it all in. She bent and traced the contours of Ria's stomach with her tongue.

Then all at once, she was on her back, Ria smiling down at her with a mischievous look. She tugged off Paige's top and easily slipped a hand underneath her, releasing the clasp of her bra with one quick motion.

"Nice technique," Paige said.

"Oh, you haven't seen anything yet."

"Big words. I hope you can back them up."

Ria quickly undid the button on Paige's jeans and tried to pull them off, but they were stuck.

"Stupid skinny jeans."

"Need some help?"

"If you wouldn't mind."

Paige sat up and tugged the ankles of her jeans free and slid out of them.

"But," Paige said, "I insist we match."

Ria quickly shed the rest of her own clothes. "Fair is fair." Paige couldn't help but admire her athletic body and the ease with which she moved. Ria helped Paige out of her remaining clothing. Then she slid a leg in between Paige's and Paige let out a sound, louder than she'd meant to. Her body ached with want.

They moved against one another, hips shifting as they fit together like puzzle pieces. Ria reached between Paige's legs and gave a smug smile at what she found.

"Oh. Well then. I think you must like me."

"Do you think so?"

Ria pushed further, sliding her fingers home, eliciting a gasp. "I think so."

Paige gripped Ria's hips tightly, digging in her fingernails, not caring if she would leave marks behind. She surrendered herself to the warmth and the pulsating color as it built upon itself until the lightning shot through her. She cried out, not caring at all what the neighbors might think.

Ria pulled her tight against her as she felt the aftershocks, kissing the side of her face.

"Well, that was a surprise," she murmured, shifting to face Ria.

Ria pretended to look at her watch. "Well," she said with a mock smirk. "I guess it's getting late. If we're done, I should probably get going."

"We are very much not done." She quickly flipped Ria onto her back.

Paige slid her fingers between Ria's thighs and felt her stomach flip at the thought that it was her that made Ria so wet there, that she wanted her that much. Ria arched her back in response. Paige kissed her, hard, and led a trail of kisses from lips to breasts to stomach, and then further. She paused, looked up at Ria.

"Yes?"

"Absolutely yes," Ria replied.

She bit the inside of Ria's thighs, rocking her hand, and then she was there, her tongue finding its home. She could feel the pressure building, felt Ria tighten underneath her until she was shouting and it was music to her ears.

"Fuck, Paige," Ria growled as the pressure finally eased. "I've been waiting my whole life for that."

They lay against each other, skin on skin, under the thin cotton sheets. Light from the street lamps came in through the blinds, streaking the room in alternating stripes.

Paige let out a deep breath.

"Is that a good sigh?" Ria asked.

"What do you think?"

"I think it's good."

"Why the hell," Paige said, "did we wait so long to do that?"

"Clearly we are idiots. We could have been doing that the whole time."

"And now you're running off to France, and leaving me here all alone. I'll have to eat French toast and French fries and watch movies with Juliette Binoche so I can imagine I'm there with you."

"You know…" Ria said, shifting against her. "You could come."

"To France?"

"Why not? Don't all artists want to paint in France?"

"Of course. We all want to wear berets and climb the Eiffel Tower and carry baguettes in our purses."

Ria gave her a light push. "I'm serious. Why not?"

Paige considered it for a second. She really couldn't think of a good reason why not. They were graduating, and she hadn't made any decisions yet about what to do next.

"Then… okay."

"Okay?"

"Why not. Let's go to France and make out along the Seine."

"That's the spirit. Let's go."

"I think you mean *allons-y*."

"See? That semester of French may actually come in handy."

"Do you really mean it?" Paige watched Ria's expression.

Ria smiled broadly. "Hell yes."

"Then I'm in."

Paige laid her head on Ria's chest and breathed in the scent of her. And before she even realized it, she was asleep.

She awoke to the sound of cars honking outside. She squinted against the sun pouring in through her window. It must be at least ten o'clock, she thought. Rolling over, she realized she was the only one in the bed.

"Ria?" she called out. No reply.

Maybe she's in the bathroom. She yawned and stretched out in her tangled sheets. Her clothes lay haphazardly on the floor next to the bed. She smiled as the night came back to her and waited for Ria to come back to bed.

After a few minutes she realized she didn't hear any noises from inside the apartment. And all Ria's clothes were gone.

Sitting upright in bed, she had a terrible thought.

No, she wouldn't do that to me. But she was already starting to worry.

She threw on a T-shirt and sweatpants and padded out into the living room. Ria's jacket was gone.

Maybe she just went out for coffee, but Paige looked around and there was no note. She grabbed her phone, but there were no messages waiting.

She took a deep breath and willed herself not to panic, but she was already starting to assume the worst.

"You idiot," she said aloud. "What did you do?"

Ria wouldn't do that. Not to her. She wouldn't use her as one of her one-night stands. Surely she was better than that.

What had she been thinking? She should have told Ria she was drunk, put her to bed on the couch, told her they would talk once she was fully sober. But she'd wanted so badly to believe everything Ria said. It was what she'd always wanted her to say.

"Fuck. Me."

She wasn't going to cry. No. She was going to shower, and then she was going to find Ria. Maybe she was getting it all wrong. Maybe Ria had to be somewhere early, and she hadn't wanted to wake her up. She just hadn't thought to leave a note behind. She shouldn't automatically assume Ria had done a "wham, bam, thank you ma'am." *And now I'm going to sneak out before you wake up and think we're in a relationship.*

An hour later she was showered and dressed and sitting at her kitchen table. Still no message from Ria. She hadn't returned with coffee or called to say *hey good morning*. Paige tried to talk herself down, but she knew she needed to talk to Ria *now*.

Moments later she was riding her bike quickly down the street toward the house Ria shared with three of her teammates. The door was unlocked when she got there, and Paige could hear voices inside. Impatiently, she opened the door and let herself in, like she had a thousand other times. Ria sat on the couch with her roommate, Sarah, and Sarah's boyfriend, playing some sort of war video game. They were shooting frantically and yelling insults at each other.

"Hey Paige!" Sarah said, noticing her in the doorway.

"Hey," she replied, trying to sound casual.

Ria looked up and smiled, but the smile didn't quite reach her eyes.

"Ria, do you have a minute?" she asked. She didn't want to talk about this with anyone else around.

"Yeah, sure. Hey Dan, take over for me for a minute?" Ria handed over her controller and walked behind Paige to the kitchen.

Once they were out of earshot, Paige turned to her.

"Ria, what the hell?"

Ria looked at her quizzically. "What?" Paige willed her to speak, but Ria just shrugged.

"What do you mean, what? You know."

"Ohhh," Ria said. "Yeah, I'm so sorry. I was so drunk when I came over last night. Man, I totally blacked out. I hope I didn't ruin your night."

"Seriously?"

"Paige, are you mad at me?"

"Are you actually trying to tell me you don't remember anything about coming over last night?"

"I know Tori dropped me off, but everything else is kind of a blur. I think I kind of overdid it."

She thought she was going to cry. Ria was obviously lying. She knew her well enough to know that. But she didn't have any idea why. Even if she really didn't remember, she would have woken up in Paige's bed and noticed the distinct lack of clothing. She would have put two and two together. The only conclusion was that Ria regretted it and wanted to pretend it never happened.

Paige stood there, hoping Ria would laugh and say she was just joking. Maybe have some excuse that she could choose to believe.

"I should probably get back to the game," Ria said. "Dan is going to get me killed."

"Right. We couldn't have that."

Ria paused for a moment, as though she was going to say something else.

Please. Please, say something.

A look passed across Ria's face and then it was gone. She smiled and gave Paige a quick kiss on the head before she turned and walked out of the room.

Paige managed to make it out of the house and around the corner before she broke down into tears.

That was the last time they'd talked, before Paige had dragged her bike into the shop a few days ago. She'd refused to pretend that nothing had happened, that Ria hadn't just ripped up their entire friendship and thrown it in the trash for a stupid one-night stand.

She couldn't forgive Ria for fooling her, for making her feel like it was safe to tell her all the secret things she'd kept to herself for years and then immediately turning and running away. Maybe it had been too much for her. Paige had wondered a lot of things, but she couldn't bring herself to confront Ria again. It was enough to know that Ria was a liar, or a coward, or both. They couldn't pretend anymore, so Paige just let it go away. She ignored Ria's texts until they stopped. Ria probably knew why because she seemed to give up a little too easily. The school year ended and Paige went off to the MFA program at UCLA. California seemed a suitable distance away from home. She didn't want to be there anymore, even though Ria was off in Europe surely having all kinds of new adventures. She didn't want to go to all the places they used to hang out, or to family gatherings at the Worths.

It wasn't just that she was angry at what Ria had done. It was that Ria had taken her best friend away, the one person who she should have been able to talk about this with. And Paige hated how much she missed her best friend.

Could they be friends again now? Had enough time passed that she could finally forgive her? *What does forgiveness mean?*

She finished sketching the flowers around the fountain and still didn't have any real answers. She'd missed Ria so much. She'd needed her so many times in their silent years, when her dad had his accident and she thought he wouldn't make it, when she'd decided to drop out of the MFA program to come home and take care of him for a while, when he'd fallen in love with one of his nurses and married her. Ria should have been there for all of that. And maybe it was Paige's own pride that kept her from making a call. Her silence had sent the message, loud and clear.

Deep inside, she knew that if Ria had just explained, just apologized, that she could have moved past it. It was too late to ask for that now, too much time had passed. So she had to decide if they could really be friends again, without that. She'd felt the lack of her so many times. And they could be friends—as long as they didn't cross that line again. With Elena here they wouldn't be tempted. Paige did not do complicated when it came to relationships.

Maybe she'd give it a little while, let their friendship have a little room to breathe, and then see how it went. She didn't have to force everything back into place right away.

As if on cue, her phone buzzed next to her. Text message. Ria. Of course.

CHAPTER EIGHT

She thought about not reading the text. She even managed to hold off for an impressive five minutes, adding some more shading to her drawing of the fountain. Then she couldn't help herself and unlocked the screen to read it.

Sorry we didn't get a chance to talk much today but so glad you came! I didn't know Elena was coming so I was surprised. You should meet her! I think you would like each other. Want to go out for drinks with us tomorrow?

That was the last thing she wanted. She wasn't sure why the thought bugged her so much. She'd never heard anything bad about Elena. If Ria was happy, she should be happy. It was just that she was excited at the chance to have her friendship back. It would be fine. Eventually.

But she still didn't want to do drinks tomorrow. Luckily, she had a good excuse.

I'm supposed to go up to Chicago tomorrow to meet with someone about the mural project. I'm so sorry! Otherwise I would love to go. It was half true.

The dots appeared on her phone immediately.

Oh how perfect! Elena hasn't seen Chicago before and I haven't had the chance to explore the city much in years. How would you feel about us driving up with you tomorrow? It's such a long, boring drive by yourself. I promise not to sing "Bohemian Rhapsody." At least, not more than a couple times at full volume. What do you say?

"Damn it," Paige said to herself. There was no easy way out of this, not that she could see.

She quickly pulled up a text string from Brandon and started typing.

What are you doing tomorrow? Want to take a road trip up to Chicago with me, Ria, and her Spanish, maybe ex-girlfriend?

The reply was immediate. *Hell yeah. Me and three women who I have absolutely zero chance with? Of course I'm in.*

At least she would have him as a buffer, if nothing else. And once they got to the city, she could go off to her meeting and let Brandon handle the rest. It would be fine. Totally fine.

CHAPTER NINE

Three and a half hours. That's how long it would take to drive from Indianapolis to Chicago, depending on traffic, speed and bathroom stops. She hoped she could make it that long without throwing herself out the window from awkwardness.

Ria had offered up her family's car for the trip. Paige would have protested, but she honestly wasn't sure if her own car would make it up and back all in one piece. She might be doing okay these days as an artist, but between making student loan payments and trying to save some money, she still had little extra to spend.

The Audi A4 was technically Mila and Henry's. Ria's own car was back at her house in Seattle, a place Paige could barely even imagine. What did Ria's life look like there? How had she decorated the house? Why even have a house when she traveled so much? And would she keep it now that she was interviewing for coaching gigs in other states? She might have asked those questions, but Elena's presence held her back.

It was like they were back to casual acquaintances, instead of having been friends since they were kids. Elena was a new X factor thrown into the mix, changing the entire equation. She just hoped Ria and Elena couldn't tell how uncomfortable she was.

Brandon offered to drive and Ria happily handed over the keys. Paige called shotgun, not quite ready to be alone with Ria or, god forbid, Elena, who somehow managed to look glamorous even in faded blue jeans, a sunny yellow tank top, and a slouchy off-white cardigan on top. Paige alternated between making idle conversation with Brandon and eavesdropping on Ria and Elena's conversation.

An hour in, they stopped to get gas and buy the unhealthy gas station snacks that can only be justified on a road trip. Elena purchased water and a packet of mixed nuts. Of course, Paige thought, as she looked down at her own choice of Diet Mountain Dew and salt and vinegar chips. She felt like such a boorish American in comparison.

"Paige," Elena said, her accent mushing up the letters of her name in a beautiful way, "would you mind trading places with me for a while? I sometimes feel a little ill in cars and sitting in the front helps."

"Oh yeah, of course. I'm so sorry, I didn't realize. The front seat is all yours." At least the girl wasn't one hundred percent perfect. She immediately felt guilty. It wasn't Elena's fault she was gorgeous and from what she could tell, really sweet as well. If Paige felt plain and a little boring, that was her own fault.

Paige climbed into the back seat as Ria got in across from her.

"Oh, I just figured you'd want to drive," she said, surprised.

"Nah," Ria replied. "Brandon seems like he's got this covered, and I'm totally fine with not having to navigate Chicago traffic."

She wasn't sure why she suddenly felt nervous and awkward. Maybe she was just anxious about her upcoming meeting with the mural's project manager. That was probably it.

Everyone buckled in and they headed back out on the highway. Ria and Paige sat in an awkward silence for a while, looking out the windows at the long stretches of farmland. Brandon and Elena immediately struck up a conversation about the windmills that dotted the landscape. He made a joke about Don Quixote and tilting at windmills that Elena seemed to find hilarious, but Paige couldn't make out the whole conversation over the music he'd put on.

"She seems nice," Paige said, breaking the silence. "Elena."

"She is," Ria said. "Though I wish I'd known she was coming to visit."

"You really didn't know she was going to be here?"

"It was a surprise. I mentioned that I'd be home for a while, and about the school dedication, but I never thought she'd actually come. She's like that, though. Adventurous. Unpredictable. Likes to go wherever the idea takes her."

"I wish I were that spontaneous," Paige said, a little wistfully. "You know I've always been a planner. I can't help it."

"I like that about you." Ria smiled. "You always have everything we need whenever we go somewhere. I bet right now you have Kleenex, quarters, a variety of writing implements, and a spare phone charger in your bag."

"I… Well, all of those things are necessities." Paige blushed. She wasn't sure why she felt embarrassed about being prepared.

"It's great. I'm better than I used to be. Constant travel for games helps. Helped, I guess. I even have a packing list of all the things I need. And…usually someone can help if—ok, when—I forget something."

"Is it going to be weird now? Not traveling with the team and a posse of support staff?"

"Probably, but I'm also looking forward to it a little. For years someone else has made my schedule—when to leave, where to go, interviews to give, practice time, photo shoots, game time, even recommendations of when to go to sleep. I'm ready to handle my own shit now, you know?"

Paige nodded, even though she couldn't really imagine all that. "I'm probably the opposite. I'm less structured than ever. When I really get into a project, I'll stay up late and sleep all day. Sometimes I won't leave my studio for a day or two. And then I pretty much sleep for days to make up for it."

"I'd love to see what you're working on sometime, if that would be ok."

"Oh." Paige stopped short. "I mean, sure. If you want to."

"I've seen some of your work—at least the concert posters and album covers. Is that mainly what you focus on now, or do you work on other projects as well?"

"I have some pieces I've been working on when I have time. I'm not sure where they're going yet, though. You're welcome to see them, if you want, as long as you know they're not quite finished. And you can get a sneak peek at the new Slurs album cover if you want. That's my main project right now, other than this mural."

They made small talk for a little while—Ria's friends from the team, Paige's art and lots of catching up on each other's families. But still, nothing too personal. And Paige definitely did not ask about Elena, or where that was going. It seemed a little too soon, and she didn't feel like she'd earned the right to ask about such personal things yet. It didn't help that when she thought about it, she felt a tiny pang of jealousy. She chalked that up to wanting to reconnect with Ria and having to share her time with someone else.

As the Chicago skyline came into view, Paige lapsed into silence. The bridge into Chicago was so huge. Its cables were thick and held the structure up high in the air. Indy was a big enough city, but it didn't have anything on this scale.

Her dad took her up to Chicago once as a kid, when he had a business trip at the same time as her fall break. He'd rolled down the window and she'd rode with her chin on the frame, amazed at the skyline and the giant bridge that spanned the gap. She'd imagined it was how New York City looked.

Ria was quiet next to her. Brandon and Elena seemed to be observing a moment of silence as well. The majesty of an engineering feat took center stage as they drove into the city.

Once across the bridge, Paige leaned forward, giving Brandon directions through the busy streets. With only a few wrong turns and close calls with speed-walking pedestrians, they rolled up next to the art gallery where Paige was to meet

Cara Bless Williams. She wondered how she should address her. Cara? Cara Bless? Ms. Williams? She didn't want to be overly formal, but she also didn't want to come off too familiar. This project was too important.

She checked her makeup and hair in a compact. Her blond locks were mostly under control in a loose bun, and she'd resisted the urge to shovel on the eyeliner. Good enough, she thought. She promised to meet the group later at Chicago Diner, her favorite restaurant in the city. She was already craving one of their cookie dough peanut butter shakes, and it was only a few blocks away from the gallery.

The outside of the building was three-story brick, the windows filled with cubed glass that made it impossible to see inside. A large wooden sign hung above the door. Mazy Gallery. Its icon was two puzzle pieces that touched but which weren't quite the right shape to connect. Paige wondered if it would be tacky to ask about the meaning behind it.

Pulling the door open, she was surprised at the darkness inside. They knew she was coming, didn't they? She turned to go back outside and double check her email. Maybe she'd remembered the time wrong, or forgotten to account for the time difference…

"Paige?" a woman's voice floated from just around the corner, past the initial darkness. "Is that you?"

"Oh, hi! Yeah, it's me."

"Come on in. Sorry, the entrance is a little dark but we're open!"

Paige walked toward the voice, keeping her arms out so she wouldn't bump into the wall—or a priceless sculpture. As she came around the corner, suddenly there was light. The main gallery was dimly lit by streams of daylight from the glass-block window. The electric lights blinked on overhead, bringing the place to a glow. The brick walls were interspersed with sections of white, each panel holding a framed painting or drawing. It was almost cozy, and it displayed the artwork well.

She stepped up to one of the paintings, a portrait of an old woman staring defiantly at the viewer. She couldn't help but stare back. The woman seemed to be challenging the viewer to judge her wrinkles, her gray hair, the age spots.

"Wow," she said aloud. The woman who walked up next to her looked like she was straight out of central casting for an art gallery owner: petite, with thick, dark hair caught up in an ornate twist. Her olive skin and strong profile added to her air of worldly glamour. She looked almost ageless, but Paige guessed she was close to forty. She wore navy cigarette pants with high heels that would have broken Paige's ankle if she'd tried to walk in them, and a gray shimmery tunic that hung on her like a model. Paige immediately wished she'd worn more than her faded black skinny jeans and a striped button-down.

"I love this one. It's part of a series by Carol Belgium. She's eighty-nine years old, and she didn't start painting until she retired. She says she's simultaneously challenging the idea that older people should just disappear and the assumption that artistic talent is something you have to be born knowing how to do."

"It's a gorgeous piece."

"I think so too. I'm Cara. It's wonderful to meet you, Paige." They shook hands, and Paige couldn't help but notice her handshake was strong, but not in a way that made her own feel weak. She'd always hated shaking hands, misjudging how still to hold her hand, how much force to use to pump the other person's up and down. It seemed like she was always showing someone a glaring character flaw in that momentary contact. But this handshake made her feel like an equal.

"Thank you," Paige replied. "I'm so glad you could meet with me today."

"You're the one who traveled hours to get here. I should be thanking you. How was your drive? I've never actually been to Indianapolis, but I know it's quite a distance away."

"It was relatively painless. I drove up with some friends and they helped make the time go by faster."

"Wonderful! Well, let me show you around my place, and then we can sit down and talk about the mural. As long as the weather holds, we can go over and see the space when we're done. Does that sound all right?"

"Sounds perfect."

Cara walked her through the gallery, periodically stopping to view a piece.

"I opened this place about three years ago. I'm originally from LA, and I worked in several galleries there, mostly contemporary art."

"Oh, I love LA. I went to UCLA there for a little over a year."

"Did you ever take classes with Dana Winter? She's a good friend of mine."

"I heard of her, but never had the chance. I ended up leaving the program a little early for family reasons."

"Ah. I got to know her when we worked on an installation together. That's mainly what I focused on out there—video and large immersive pieces. In those days it was all about pushing the boundaries of what was called art. But eventually I started to circle back to pieces that were more permanent. Paintings, drawings, sculptures have a timeless feel, even when the subject matter is daring."

"How did you end up in Chicago? It's so different than LA."

Cara laughed. "For the reason so many of us move to a place we never would have expected. Love. I followed a woman I thought was the love of my life. She was an architect and was working on a project in LA. We met at one of my gallery openings, and I was immediately smitten. Of course, if I'd known she was from such a cold and windy place, I might have focused my attentions elsewhere." She smiled.

"But by the time I knew she was from halfway across the country, it was too late. I would have followed her anywhere. I pulled up my roots, took a job at the Art Institute, and bought some coats and sweaters. It's a wonderful museum, have you been?" Paige nodded. "But smaller galleries really are my passion. And when my partner and I divorced, I took my half of the money and bought this place."

"Oh," Paige said. "I'm so sorry. About the divorce, I mean. The place is beautiful."

Cara waved her hands. "Passion doesn't always last. I have no regrets. And it brought me here. I would probably never have come on my own. All this...weather! But, it's where I belong. And there is a different quality to the art being made here. It's more...heartfelt, I think, than some of the work I was encountering back in LA. It's not about making a splash, attracting celebrity attention, hoping to land on Angelina Jolie's wall. Or at least, not the work that I represent. I search for work that has strong technique and that also reaches through the medium to touch you, whether that's to tell you something, scream at you, make you sad, or bring you joy. These days, I search for work that tells personal stories that are also about the broader world."

As Cara talked, Paige listened, enraptured. It was like she was speaking a language Paige had been trying to find the words for all along. She could have listened to it all day. She'd forgotten how much she loved talking about art. Her friends in Indy were creative types, but they were more into music, like Brandon, or theater or writing. It was close, but not the same.

"Now, the mural project," Cara continued. "That's not only my project. It was the committee's—artists, gallery owners, city officials, and community representatives. Quite the mixed bag of bureaucrats and art folk. We all had to agree on the design. And we're not supposed to reveal how everyone voted but..." She leaned over conspiratorially. "Yours was the one everyone couldn't stop talking about. At first I was a little skeptical of the theme we selected. "Home in the Midwestern City" just sounded so... generic. But it was a starting point, and you never know what artists will create when you give them a beginning kernel. I'm always in support of public art, whether or not I like the piece. It creates discussion and adds visual interest to the otherwise utilitarian city."

"I agree," Paige said. "In Indianapolis, the main branch of the public library has what looks like a giant chocolate donut attached to it. I have no idea what it's about. And I haven't tried to find out because I love the incongruity of it. I prefer imagining why someone created a chocolate donut sculpture to go on such a stately building, and thinking about all the layers of approvals it had to go through to become a permanent fixture."

Cara smiled. "Exactly. Perhaps you can show me this chocolate donut if I visit Indianapolis sometime?"

"I'd be happy to," Paige said, though the idea of showing Cara around her hometown was a little intimidating.

Cara led Paige back to a small office, where they sat down at a beautifully restored 1920's secretary desk to talk about the logistical details of the mural. They discussed materials and equipment, the best dates to begin painting if weather cooperated, and accommodations for Paige's stay during that time.

"I do want to talk about evolving your piece a little more. I love it, but I think once you see the space you'll want to make a few changes. Are you ready to go see where the piece will have its home?"

"Absolutely."

"Perfect. Then just one moment while I change my shoes."

Paige was relieved. She'd been trying to imagine how anyone could walk on those towering heels through the streets of Chicago without tripping.

Cara opened a desk drawer and pulled out a pale blue pair of Keds. Paige almost laughed. She had not expected that. She immediately thought back to all the pairs of Keds she'd worn throughout childhood, in various colors and designs. Who knew that Keds were so uncool that they were cool again? Or perhaps Cara could just make everything seem effortlessly stylish.

Locking the door behind them, Cara led her through the city, narrating its history along the way. For such a recent transplant, she had gathered up information about her new home quickly. Paige imagined that was part of what made her so successful—being interested in everything and everyone around her, collecting it all and sharing the information forward.

Finally, Cara stopped and pointed up. It was Paige's wall. She'd seen it online, of course, but seeing it now in person, it looked so…huge. She breathed deeply. This was where her work was going to live. Four stories high, towering above the people walking past. How many people would see her piece every single day as they walked to work, home, on dates, out shopping? It would become a little piece of their lives, whether they thought about it or not. She couldn't help it. One tear escaped and then another.

Cara smiled at her but didn't say anything. She gave her the moment without commentary, seeming to understand why Paige was crying.

It was as though her whole life had led her here. Every dead end, every misstep, argument, or crumpled up drawing brought her to this wall, which was now hers to adorn. Her art would cover it until the wind and rain and snow slowly eroded it years into the future. And even that would be part of the perfect cycle of life.

When she told Cara that she was meeting her friends at Chicago Diner, Cara insisted on walking with her.

"I want to know more about you," she said. So Paige told her she'd always drawn as a kid, about the great art teachers in junior high and high school that encouraged her, and walked her through her style and subject matter evolution. Cara nodded and smiled, asking questions that kept her talking about herself and her work.

"There is a question I like to ask artists when I meet them for the first time," Cara said. "I know it puts you on the spot, but I'd like know: What has been the most meaningful piece you have created to date? Not necessarily the one that received the most praise, brought in the most money, or is the best known, but the one that is closest to your heart."

"*That* is a tough question to answer," Paige said, thinking over the work she'd created in the past decade and a half.

"The best ones are, I think."

She didn't have to think long. "I did this painting my first year at UCLA. It was about the violence of love. I made the phrase 'tear my heart out' literal. For the first time, I wasn't trying to just vaguely reference emotions or events—it was front and center. I took my characters, two girls in the middle of the painting, and they had their hands in each other's chest, holding their hearts, pulling them out with strings of blood behind them. It was the most visceral thing I've painted, even though I didn't break from the glossy figures and the doll-like eyes that people tend to associate with me. Obviously, I was dealing with some pretty major heartbreak, and at the time I just wanted to get it out onto canvas."

"I'd love to see it," Cara said.

"I wish you could. At the time I felt like I wanted to get it all out of me, and then get rid of it. I didn't keep any of the sketches or even take photos of the final piece. I did a summer abroad in Florence and the last week there I hung it in a group show. It sold, and I don't even know who bought it. I've tried to track it down a couple times, but no one has posted it online, so it's probably gathering dust in someone's basement now."

"That's awful."

"Well, it taught me a lesson—always document everything. And maybe it was meant to be ephemeral."

"I appreciate you sharing that with me. I love to watch people's faces as they talk about their work, and I can see how deeply you feel about yours. If you bring a fraction of that to this mural, it will be absolutely stunning."

They were a few doors down from the restaurant now.

"Thank you, Cara," Paige said. "I really look forward to working with you on this. I'm so glad to have the opportunity."

"Oh Paige," Cara laughed. "I think we'll be the lucky ones."

Cara gave her a light hug as they said their goodbyes and turned to leave.

She turned back. "Don't forget!" she called. "I still want to see that chocolate donut."

Paige smiled. All she wanted to do was get home and get to work on revising her sketches for the mural. Cara was right. After seeing the immensity of the space she had to work with, she wanted to expand on her original idea. But first, she needed to get through dinner and the long drive home.

CHAPTER TEN

"How was it?" Ria asked, as Paige slid into the diner's booth across from her.

"It was really great." Paige felt like she was walking on air, and she didn't have the words to describe to everyone at the table everything she was feeling. Maybe to Ria or Brandon alone, but not to the group of three. "What were you all up to while I was doing work things?"

"We played tourist," Brandon said. "Since this was Elena's first time in Chicago, of course we had to go to the Bean."

"Oh, I love the Bean," Paige replied. "Elena, what did you think?"

"It was so shiny! I don't know why there is a giant metal jelly bean in the middle of the city but I like it." Paige nodded. She'd just been saying the same thing about the donut on the Indianapolis library. Maybe Elena wasn't so bad after all.

Elena pulled out her phone and flipped through the photos they'd taken posing against the famed attraction. Paige noticed

Elena photographed just as beautifully as she looked in real life. *Some people just have all the luck.*

"And then we rode the ferris wheel," Ria added. "Elena's afraid of heights, but she was a trooper."

"It was not so high!" Elena insisted. "I was not scared with my friends there."

Brandon grinned. He'd always had a knack for making quick friends of anyone he met, but he clearly was proud to be considered a friend of a well-known athlete and her gorgeous girlfriend from Spain.

Paige's stomach growled audibly, and she sheepishly looked up at the group.

"Did you order yet?"

"We were waiting for you, but we can be ready," Ria promised. She waved at the server and he walked over with the practiced gait of one who is too cool to hustle but still wants a good tip.

"What is the best thing here that we should order?" Elena asked, clearly preferring the staff suggestion over picking one of the menu options at random.

He glanced at her and blushed. Paige mentally rolled her eyes. Beautiful people are just different than the rest of us, she thought. At least having Elena at their table meant they'd get great service.

"Oh, um, well, the seitan reuben is really popular. And any of our milkshakes. We have some really great pie too."

He stammered over his words so much that Paige almost felt sorry for him. Ria caught her eye and they shared bemused glances. Elena took it all in stride, clearly used to unnerving men—and women—everywhere she went. Paige wondered what it was like to have that kind of effect on people. She was glad people didn't fall all over her, but it was probably nice sometimes to have people rushing to please you.

"Wonderful. I will have one, and a cup of herbal tea. Perhaps I will try the pie afterward," Elena pronounced, handing her menu over to the flustered server.

"One of…what? I'm sorry," he replied.

"One roo-ben," Elena said, "and whatever is your favorite pie. You choose, I trust you."

"Oh, um, okay. Great." He closed his notepad and started to turn away, then abruptly realized he hadn't taken anyone else's order. He laughed at himself and opened the pad again.

Ria ordered a mushroom burger. Brandon followed with a sandwich they called a "seitan-derloin," a play on the popular Midwestern staple tenderloins, and then it was Paige's turn. As the resident vegetarian of the group, she struggled over all the options available. It was so rare to visit a place where she could eat everything on the menu. That's why this was her favorite restaurant, even though she only came here every few years. She imagined this was like the average person's experience at Applebee's. She envied their ability to read through pages and pages of options, all available to them, while she scoured the lists of ingredients for a single thing she could eat, often settling for wilted lettuce and a side of French fries.

This place, in comparison, was paradise. Six beautiful pages of vegetarian entrees, sides, and desserts, beautifully photographed and lovingly described. It was like a man in the desert walking for miles, finding an oasis, and being offered twelve different flavors of water. How to choose one over the other when you're so thirsty?

Finally she chose one. Mushroom, lentil, and veggie "meet" loaf, with mashed potatoes, beets, and agave-glazed carrots. She could have drooled just reading that description. Perfect comfort food after an amazing day, nourishing her stomach after her spirit felt fulfilled. Maybe that was dramatic hyperbole, but for once she was willing to indulge.

As the server collected their menus and left, Paige felt her phone vibrate in her pocket. Surreptitiously she checked the text under the table.

It was wonderful to meet you today, Paige. I look forward to working with you on this project. The city will be even more inspiring with your work on its surface. Safe travels and we will speak again soon.

Paige couldn't help but grin and she didn't try to hide it. She hadn't felt this happy in a very long time.

"All good?" Ria asked.

"The best."

CHAPTER ELEVEN

They were all full, even the ever-carnivorous Brandon praising the hearty food and the perfectly crafted desserts. It was night by the time they put themselves back in the car and began their journey back south.

Paige volunteered to drive and Ria called shotgun. Elena and Brandon happily took the backseat, chattering like they were old friends.

"They keep talking about something called 'early music,'" Ria whispered conspiratorially. "Apparently they're both fans of music that is not late." The two in the backseat were deep in conversation and paid her no mind.

"Really? I knew Brandon liked that stuff. Well, that and hardcore screaming metal. He's a man of many interests. But I didn't realize anyone else under the age of eighty-two, or at least a music teacher like Brandon, was even aware it was a genre of music."

"I guess I've heard her playing it before, but I always just assumed it was music to do yoga to. Not something to listen to on purpose."

"I call it monk music," Paige said.

"It's not monk music," Brandon called from the backseat.

"Oh, it's definitely what a monk would rock out to," Ria retorted. "Headbanging, stomping their feet, chanting, and all that. Just, you know, unplugged."

"Whatever," Brandon said, going back to his conversation with Elena. Paige heard him say something about Anne Boleyn and immediately tuned out.

"I tried painting to it a couple times," Paige said to Ria. "I thought maybe it would mellow me out, make me concentrate. But mostly, it made me want to nap."

The radio hissed as it lost its Chicago station signal. Ria turned the dial until she found a station playing old 90's hip-hop. Brandy and Monica were singing "The Boy Is Mine."

"I had this CD when we were kids," Ria said. "Do you remember?"

"I loved this song. Of course I changed it in my head to 'The Girl Is Mine'."

"Of course you did."

The conversation continued behind them. It was as though Brandon and Elena had known each other for years.

"He's an interesting guy, your roommate," Ria said. "Covered in tattoos, towering over people, tight T-shirts, but then—boom—he starts belting out opera in the middle of Chicago."

"He did that?"

"Elena dared him to, right by the Bean. I got a video. I think a bunch of tourists did too. He's really good, actually."

"I know. I've told him he should go to New York or somewhere with something bigger than the Indianapolis Opera, but I think he likes his job teaching the classical vocalist students at Butler. He only teaches three days a week and offers private lessons on the side."

"Ah, that makes sense. I wondered how he could get up and leave during the day to drive up to Chicago with us."

"It's not a bad gig, for sure."

"We should introduce him to my brother the next time he's back in town. They'd probably have tons to talk about. How did you meet him? I wouldn't guess you ran in the same circles."

"Eh. It seems like all the circles in Indianapolis overlap at some point. But we met when I came back from school when my dad got hurt. He's one of the leaders of this fitness group that meets every Wednesday. It's a free group workout once a week, way too early in the morning. I started going to get out some of the stress. And he was so friendly. It made it actually fun to wake up at five a.m. and run the stairs at the War Memorial. Then when I decided to move back for good, he needed a roommate and the rest is history."

"Early history? Or late history?"

"Definitely late post-modern chaos theory latter-day history."

"So, totally off-topic, how is your dad these days? I've been wanting to ask."

"He's actually really good. The accident turned out to have a silver lining, if you can call it that. The company that owned the semi that hit his car offered a pretty generous settlement and he was finally able to retire. He only limps a little, though he definitely complains about being able to feel the weather in his bad leg. And of course, he met Celia. They're pretty great together."

"That's awesome," Ria said. "Not that he got hurt, but that it turned out all right for him."

"You know, I think he didn't date when I was a kid because he didn't want me to think he was trying to replace my mom. And then he was used be being alone. I tried to get him to sign up for Match.com one time but he told me that no way was I going to sell him off on the internet."

"That sounds like him."

"Yeah."

The conversation in the back seat had died down. Paige glanced in the rearview mirror and saw that both Brandon and Elena had fallen asleep.

Paige and Ria watched as the midnight-dark world sped past them, as though they were alone in a tiny pod hurtling through space.

Paige eased the car into Ria's driveway, all three of her passengers asleep. For the last hour, she'd been the only one awake, alone with only her thoughts and a podcast of *Wait, Wait, Don't Tell Me* to keep her going. She'd thought about stopping and asking Brandon to switch with Ria to keep her awake, but they all looked so peaceful.

She parked just outside the garage.

"Good morning, sunshines. You don't have to go home, and you can stay here if you want to. Except for Brandon. You actually do have to go home, because your car is here and it's my ride."

The sleeping trio blinked back into consciousness.

"Oh wow, Paige, I'm so sorry," Ria said. "I didn't mean to fall asleep."

"It's okay. I think you needed it."

Ria unbuckled her seatbelt and yawned. "What time is it?" she asked, glancing at her phone. "Oh wow, it's one a.m. I have to be on a plane in seven hours."

Paige startled. "You're leaving already? You didn't tell us that."

"I told you. I have interviews for coaching jobs."

"Oh. Yeah, I just didn't realize you meant tomorrow, or I guess, today. Wow. If I'd realized I wouldn't have dragged you all the way up to Chicago."

"You didn't drag me at all. Actually, I'm pretty sure it was my idea. And it was a lot of fun, so I'm glad we went."

"Where are you off to?"

"Universities of Tennessee, Virginia, and…North Carolina."

"North Carolina? Seriously? Ria, that's incredible. I mean, any of them would be but that's…" Paige whistled.

"Well, I definitely don't have the job yet. And they're just for assistant coaching positions, not that they're any less important. We'll see how it goes."

"Talk about burying the lede," Paige said, shaking her head. "You're just full of surprises. Promise me you'll tell me how it goes?"

"Sure, I promise. When there's something to tell, you'll be the first to know."

"After Henry and Mila," Paige warned. "Don't get me in trouble here."

Brandon and Elena had climbed out of the backseat and were sleepily leaning against the car.

"You ready, Brandon?" Paige asked. He responded with a wide-mouthed yawn. "Sounds like a yes."

The group hugged in pairs. Ria embraced Paige warmly as Brandon and Elena hugged. *They sure bonded quickly. I guess early music fans have to stick together.* Elena stepped forward to hug Paige. Paige put an arm around her stiffly, but tried to relax into it, telling herself to stop being awkward. Brandon gave Ria a quick hug, and then pretended he was about to give one to Paige too.

"Oh right," he joked. "I'm keeping this one."

On the twenty-minute drive back to their apartment, Paige stared out the window, letting the day wash over her. So many miles traveled and so much still to do. She was ready to get to work on the final design of her mural. But first, sleep.

Once they made it home and walked up the stairs to their second-floor apartment, Brandon turned to Paige with a funny look on his face.

"Thanks for inviting me today. I had a really good time."

Paige hit him lightly. "Thank you for coming. You made everything so much easier. And you know, I love to learn more about early music."

She quickly brushed her teeth and tugged off her jeans. She landed on her bed, threw the blanket over herself, and slept the hardest she had in months.

CHAPTER TWELVE

It seemed like the morning sun came up sooner than usual. She checked the clock. Nine a.m. Ria would already be on a flight taking her several states away. It was probably for the best. It had been nice reconnecting with her, but now with Elena back in the picture, Paige and Ria probably wouldn't have spent much time together anyway.

It was time to get to work. After seeing the future home of her mural yesterday and talking with Cara, she could feel her brain churning, working through the ideas and evolving her first concept into something even more.

Did she smell coffee? She yawned and pushed herself out of bed, padded out of her bedroom into the apartment's kitchen.

There was at least enough left for one cup, the coffee's aroma intoxicating to someone who had only slept a few hours. Brandon had left a note beside it: *Volunteered to take Ria to the airport so her parents could sleep in. Thought you might need this when you woke up.*

She shook her head and smiled a tired smile. He was one of the good ones. It was sweet of him to volunteer to drive Ria, even though it was almost certainly out of his way. She felt a little guilty that she hadn't got up to join him, but not that bad. Involuntarily she yawned again and emptied the pot into her cup.

After a quick shower, she dressed in her usual uniform of paint-splattered jeans and an old T-shirt from the MoMA gift shop in New York. It was faded, but she loved how it had thinned wash after wash until it was soft against her skin.

She took her bike off its wall mount in the living room, gathered her bag, and carried the bike down to the street. It was ten a.m. on a weekday and the city was already awake and at work as she rode toward her studio. Her stomach rumbled, warning her that she'd better eat something if she was going to work all day. She stopped at General American Donut, though the fried sugary dough probably wasn't the most nutritional fuel. The place felt like home. She'd worked there a few years ago, the super early morning shift making the donuts, before the sun was up and anyone else was awake. Sometimes she missed it—the calmness of the motions, over and over, nothing but music or a podcast over the speaker, alone in the world. It had been bittersweet when she was finally making enough money from her art to quit the job, but the owners had been kind about it. They even had a small drawing of hers framed behind the counter.

Enough delay, she thought, and put the bag of donuts along with her newly refilled coffee tumbler into her bike's basket and rode to her studio.

She carried her bike up the stairs to her second-floor workspace. Unloading all her belongings, she turned to look at the mural sketches taped up on the walls. She was ready to work.

Her original idea was good. It was always interesting to look at her creations after some time had passed and to be surprised at how much she actually liked them, especially because they were never exactly the way she saw them in her head.

She'd first come across the mural project when she was skimming the list of calls for submission the Arts Commission put out each week. When she'd first read the theme, "Making Home in the Midwestern City," it hadn't really spoken to her, but she'd bookmarked it in case she thought of something later. It had sounded kind of bland, like one of those ubiquitous Thomas Kincaid paintings sold at stores in the mall. Not that she was knocking Thomas Kincaid. He was making bank, and Paige's dad loved his depictions of churches in nature glowing with light.

Making home made her think of homemakers, and she didn't know much about that. She'd never been particularly domestic, and growing up with just her and Dad, dinner was made in the microwave more often than not. Like many of her projects, the idea percolated just under the layer of her consciousness. Sometimes they would come to the surface and she'd start to work; sometimes they would disappear.

It was only three days before the deadline that the thought came to her: *Whose* home in the city? The city was made up of so many different people, all going in different directions, driving, taking the bus, biking, walking, shopping, going to school, working, passing by each other. That's what made it a city, the invisible webs woven by all that activity. And that's what she decided to draw.

She used her characters, colorful and manga-like Botticelli figures, placed them in cars and buses, on bikes and skateboards, and showed their movements through city streets with ribbons trailing behind them, braiding together as they crossed each other's paths. The ribbons formed the outline of a house in the center of the piece. It looked fantastical, and almost like a board game, a modern mash-up of Candyland meets The Game of Life.

She'd bought a large, cheap canvas, almost as tall as she was, and created her piece on it. Then she took a photo from across the room and emailed it in with her application. Other people's submissions probably looked cleaner, but in the end they had chosen hers. Luckily people in the art world were used to artists having their quirks.

It was good, she thought, standing back and looking at it, but the drive up to Chicago had given her an idea. All around the cities, both Indy and Chicago, the land was pushing up crops. Corn, soy, tomatoes, it rose in green stalks and tendrils for miles all around.

The piece needed a frame. Paige began sketching corn stalks, thick on the page, their leaves reaching up, then arcing back toward the ground, husks emerging between them. Atop each one the tassels waved in an imaginary breeze. The city wasn't separate from its surroundings; it was connected to them too, just like the people in the city were connected in ways they would probably never realize. They were all pieces of one web, one machine, one world.

She worked furiously throughout the day and into the night, finally dozing off on the futon in one corner. When she woke, she looked up at the thrift store clock leaning up against the wall to check the time. She thought for the hundredth time that she should really get around to mounting it. Seven thirty. The light outside was pale, and for a moment, she wasn't sure if it was a.m. or p.m. It felt like she was in between worlds, timeless.

Sketches in various states of completion lay all around or taped to the wall. This mural was such a different process. She knew they would project it bigger than she drew it, so that it would fill the whole wall, but that meant she had to visualize the whole picture in her head.

She hoped Cara would like the new elements. She had seemed open to whatever she imagined. It was nice that they'd chosen a gallery owner to spearhead the project instead of a city bureaucrat. She seemed to understand the practicalities without asking Paige to compromise her vision for the sake of what paint colors might be on sale, or what a focus group would ask her to change.

She stretched and listened as her body cracked. That must have been the sign that she was finally awake because her stomach growled loudly. Whether it was seven thirty a.m. or p.m., she hadn't eaten in hours. She grabbed her phone and wallet and wandered out of the building toward the greasy spoon that had been in the neighborhood forever and would probably outlast them all. It was open twenty-four hours, which was perfect for her schedule when she was deep in a project.

Two old men sat outside on a picnic table smoking. They were fixtures there, regardless of the time of day or the season. A little consistency was nice, even if smoking seemed incongruous now. As the neighborhood was gaining trendy restaurants and adding new coats of paint to once-neglected buildings, this little place was still holding its ground.

Paige opened the door and was immediately greeted by the scent of fried potatoes and diner coffee. It felt like home. They would never judge her in here for the bird-nest state of her hair or the paint on her arms, if they even noticed at all.

She grabbed the booth closest to the door, her favorite one. The plastic cushions were cracked from decades of butts sitting on them and the Formica tabletop was chipped in all the right places.

Maybe I should draw this place someday, she thought. She imagined her creatures sitting in the booths. What would they eat?

Once she'd ordered a massive breakfast, she looked at her phone. When she worked, she put it on vibrate, but she couldn't bring herself to power down completely. Ever since her dad's accident, she felt like she needed to be reachable, just in case, even though he was married and had someone else to be his emergency contact now. But only her dad's and Celia's messages and calls were programmed to ring through when she was working. Everything else could wait.

Her last serious girlfriend hadn't appreciated that. Laura was an engineer, and she just thought more logically. She didn't like it when Paige disappeared into a project, though she tried to understand. Paige supposed it was hard on Laura when Paige needed to be alone with her thoughts and her tools. She'd tried dating other artists, but their individual quirks added up to way too much difficulty.

It wasn't that she didn't want a relationship. She just wanted one that didn't mean she had to give up something she loved, if that was possible. Everyone said relationships were compromise, but some things were too important. Or maybe she was just stubborn. Anyhow, no one had ever made her want to really reevaluate the way she lived her life.

There were multiple messages on her phone. A couple texts from Ria and an email from Cara. Damn, when had she become so popular? She felt a quiver in her stomach, but that could have just been from hunger. As if he knew, her server dropped off a plate of loaded hash browns and she dug in.

She read Ria's texts first.

11:30 a.m.: *Landed safely in Knoxville! Thanks for a really great trip to Chicago. I'm so sorry I fell asleep on the way home!*

6 p.m.: *Knoxville is good so far, not that I've seen much more than my hotel and the campus, but the stadium's nice. They seem like good people. Not sure if this is the one, but we'll see if they make me an offer.*

11 p.m.: *Headed to bed. Hope you're having a productive day of work! I'm off to Charlottesville tomorrow for interview #2.*

Now that she was awake and a little more aware, Paige realized it was indeed morning, so she decided to wait a while to text Ria back.

She was a little nervous about reading Cara's email. What if she'd changed her mind or thought Paige's ideas were boring and lame? That was ridiculous, she knew it, but she wondered if she would ever get to the point where she was as confident as other people seemed.

Dear Paige. Paige always thought the formality of letters was funny. Even before they'd met they referred to each other as dear.

I am so inspired by your visit. I hate to pressure you, though I suppose that's what project managers do, right? We pressure you to meet deadlines, and you make us tear our hair out by missing the deadlines or making us think you're going to. And in the end it all comes together and we show beautiful art.

But back to the pressure I just mentioned. Next week I am due to visit an artist in Louisville, and instead of going there directly, I thought I would stop in Indianapolis and check in with you along the way. Don't panic! I know your mind is moving a million miles a second right now with new ideas. I look forward to seeing whatever you have on paper by the time I arrive.

If you have time while I'm there, I would love to take you to dinner. You choose the restaurant. It's on the gallery's tab, so choose anywhere you like. When you have time, please let me know if you are able to accommodate my surprise trip. I do hope so!

It was such a pleasure to meet you, and I truly look forward to this project.

Sincerely,
Cara Bless Williams

Paige's mouth hung open, a bite of potatoes held aloft on her fork. Next week? Her stomach knotted at the prospect. She had only a few days to ready her sketches for Cara to see. And maybe she should do something about her hair. Her highlights were so grown out she looked like a lazy tiger.

Why was she worrying about her hair? This was just about work. Cara didn't care what she looked like. Although...she had invited her to dinner. But on the gallery's tab. It was business.

Right, Paige, she thought, because no one ever mixes business with pleasure. That's why it's an expression. No, she was just sleep-deprived. She needed to focus. Cara was coming to Indianapolis next week, and she needed to be ready. She wolfed down the rest of her breakfast, drank down her coffee, and dropped cash on the table to cover her bill. There was no time to waste.

CHAPTER THIRTEEN

She checked her phone for the time, and once she glanced away, promptly forgot it and had to check again. Paige couldn't remember the last time she'd been this nervous. It was even worse than when she'd met Cara in Chicago, because now that she knew her, and they'd been emailing and texting since then, Cara's positive opinion seemed that much more important. It was irrational because Cara had sent nothing but praise and a few perfect suggestions. But what if she saw the sketches in person and decided they weren't right after all?

What if it wasn't that Paige was nervous about her work, but something else instead? Their texts had started to veer from just about the project into everything else, from food to where they grew up, to the embarrassing TV shows they secretly loved. But Paige didn't want to read something into it that wasn't there. This project mattered too much.

Cara was late. She'd probably hit some traffic on the way down. It was hard to miss rush hour, either in Chicago or Indy, if you didn't time it just right.

The phone chimed. *I'm here. Should I come up?*

Paige took a deep breath. *Be right down to get you.*

She looked around the studio. She'd tried to neaten the place up a little, but messy was her natural state, so she'd only been somewhat successful. Her sketches were laid out across the table and clipped to the wall. Breathe, she told herself. Why was she so damn nervous? She'd met Joan Jett at a musical festival once and was totally fine, mostly, but she was almost shaking right now. Steadying herself as best she could, she left the studio and went downstairs to greet Cara.

How was it possible that Cara was even more gorgeous today, when she'd been driving for hours? Paige opened her mouth to say hello and fumbled for worlds. Oh god, this is embarrassing, she thought.

Cara breezily leaned in to give her a hug. She smelled wonderful, like a light but expensive perfume. Paige wondered if it was obvious that she'd labored over what to wear. Her bed back at the apartment was covered in the clothes she'd tried on and discarded before going with her usual uniform of a button-down shirt and jeans, but adding a tweed vest on top to dress it up. Everything else she'd tried on felt like a costume, and she needed to feel like herself.

Cara wore a navy jumpsuit, cinched at the waist with a white shrug covering her shoulders. Paige had always privately made fun of people who wore jumpsuits, since they seemed like they would make going to the bathroom impractical. But on Cara, it looked like it had been made for her to wear. Large round sunglasses made her look even more the classic movie star in the afternoon's fading sun.

"It's so good to see you." Cara said. Her hair hung down in loose curls, and Paige imagined what it would feel like against her cheek.

Get it together, Paige.

"It's good to see you too. Please, come up."

They walked close together up the stairs. "How was your drive down?"

"As nice as a long drive can be. It gave me time to listen to an audiobook. I really only listen to them when I drive, and I drive so rarely in Chicago."

"Oh, what book are you listening to?"

"It's about Julia Child. Apparently she was a sort-of spy during World War II. It's very interesting. Not so much about her cooking."

"I might have to check it out." She knew she never would. She couldn't focus on audiobooks and by the time she realized her thoughts had drifted off, she'd always lost too much of the plot.

They stood awkwardly for a few moments. Why was this so hard? Paige hoped Cara didn't notice. It felt so strange to have her here in her studio. It was like a fairy showing up in your living room, too unreal to be believed.

"Can I look?" Cara asked.

"Oh, of course! Please." Paige was embarrassed. Cara was here to look at the art. Why was she making it weird?

She went to the table and thumbed through the sketches, considering each one before moving on. Once through the stack on the table, she walked around the room, pausing at each piece clipped to the wall. She didn't say anything while she looked, and Paige's stomach turned over slowly. Finally she turned to Paige, her face serious. Then, like a ray of sunshine, a smile broke across her face.

"It's wonderful," she said. "So much more than I'd hoped for. You really have a gift."

"Thank you so much." A wave of relief passed through her. "I'm so glad you think it's right for the project."

"It's going to be my favorite piece of public art in the city," Cara declared. "But there's just one question."

"Oh. What's that?"

"Where do we go for dinner?"

CHAPTER FOURTEEN

Paige had walked past Cerulean so many times, but she had never been inside. Fancy restaurants had never really been her thing, and she couldn't justify paying so much for such small plates of food. But Cara had done her research, or at least read some Yelp reviews, and decided that this would be the perfect place for her first dinner in Indianapolis.

The moment they walked inside, Paige immediately felt underdressed. Maybe she should have worn a dress or her one pair of black slacks. Cara, of course, fit in with ease. The lighting was dim, and they followed a hostess to a booth that offered plenty of privacy. The hostess disappeared as they sat, then immediately reappeared with a frosted glass bottle of water, which she poured while telling them that their server, Keith, would be by in just a moment.

Colorful teardrop glass lamps hung overhead, and Paige wondered if she could afford one of them. The other half lived quite well, she thought, though she wasn't sure which half she was, or if she was straddling the line. Growing up with Ria's family, she'd known they'd had money, but they didn't go out to places like this.

Keith arrived and handed them each a menu, arranged as a small sheaf of papers clipped together.

"We're celebrating," Cara told him before he'd had a chance to tell them about the chef's signature dish. She ordered a bottle of wine with a name that Paige would never be able to pronounce, and Keith poured them each a glass before saying he would give them time to look over the menu.

Cara raised her glass and Paige raised hers in response.

"A toast," Cara said, "to making art and making connections."

Paige smiled and clinked her glass against Cara's. She made everything look so effortless. Paige felt the wine flow through her and warm her blood. If this is the life, she thought, it's not bad. Not bad at all.

Keith reappeared, and with a flourish, offered them an amuse-bouche from the chef. Paige looked down and tried not to laugh. It was half a mushroom on a little wooden block. For the two of them to share. If Ria had been there, they would have mocked the pretension, but next to Cara, she tried to act as though half a mushroom was a completely normal thing to be offered.

Sipping more wine, Paige's nerves finally began to relax. She and Cara laughed and talked about Cara's next show and the play she'd been to see the week before. Keith presented several dishes of food artfully stacked in the center of white china, the sauces drizzled in swirls around them. As they debated ordering dessert, Paige felt Cara's foot touch hers. She wasn't sure if it was an accident or possibly something else. The last thing she wanted to do was cross a line and assume something that wasn't there.

They shared a thick slice of chocolate cake, and once there was nothing but crumbs left, Keith presented a check, which Cara immediately scooped up. Paige tried to split the tab with her, but Cara reminded her this was the gallery's treat. Paige didn't fight her very hard, catching sight of a bill that had more digits than she'd ever spent on a single meal. But this was a celebration. And Cara was seeing the finer aspects of life in Indy. Paige was glad for that. Whenever she traveled, people assumed there was nothing but football and cornfields in Indiana, and she was always trying to tell them that it was that, but also so much more.

It was a beautiful night, and Paige didn't want it to end yet. She suggested walking through downtown. Cara quickly agreed.

For an almost-summer night, it wasn't too hot so they took the Cultural Trail toward White River State Park. It seemed like everyone was out tonight. A few teenagers practiced dance steps in a grassy area just off the street and they paused to watch them.

"Did you ever take dance?" Cara asked.

"No," Paige said. "I never really took any lessons. I played soccer as a kid for a few years, but that was the only physical thing I did. I was pretty obsessed with drawing from the time I was little. Did you dance?"

"I wanted to be a ballerina," she replied. "I thought they were so elegant and beautiful."

"I could see you as a ballerina. What stopped you?"

"To be honest, I simply wasn't good enough. I rehearsed constantly but I rarely got a solo. It's a sad thing, not to be good at what we love, or at least not good enough, when there is so much competition. I knew eventually that it wasn't going to be a career for me. But I still love to dance."

"I'm so sorry. That realization must have been heartbreaking."

"It was. But in the end I found my place. I wouldn't trade where I am for anything. Except the lead in Swan Lake, perhaps." She smiled and Paige couldn't help but return it.

They passed couples sitting on benches and leaning against walls. It was as though the night had called out to all those in a romantic mood to bring them here. Paige sensed Cara's presence as she walked so near to her, occasionally brushing the fabric of her clothing against her when they turned, or touching her lightly when one of them said something funny.

They reached the end of the path and paused, not quite ready to turn around. The electricity between them was building steadily, and Paige was so aware of the tingling in her fingertips and the flush of her skin. Cara touched Paige's arm lightly with her fingertips and looked up at her. Paige smiled back nervously.

"Would you mind if I kissed you?" Cara asked.

Paige felt her stomach drop. This was real. "Please do," she said, her voice nearly a whisper. She pulled Cara to her, their lips meeting, softly at first, and then more. They tangled their fingers in each other's hair and lost themselves in this perfect, magical night.

Who knew how long they would have gone on. Someone whistled at them from afar and they quickly broke apart.

Cara laughed. "I nearly forgot we were in public."

"Maybe we should go somewhere else," Paige replied, a little breathlessly.

"My hotel room is all the way up on Eighty-Sixth Street by Fashion Mall," Cara said.

"My apartment is only a few minutes away."

"I'd love to see your apartment," Cara grinned.

Paige suspected the only room they would spend any time in was the bedroom, and she was just fine with that.

CHAPTER FIFTEEN

Paige turned the key in the lock, feeling a little self-conscious, but buoyed by the night and the wine and that kiss. She wished she would have hung up her clothes earlier and not left them all over the bed, but she didn't think Cara would mind if she just pushed them to the floor.

Cara leaned in and kissed her as Paige pushed the door open and they stepped inside. Paige nearly tripped over something lying by the door and cursed lightly under her breath. She didn't remember leaving anything there, but she wasn't known for her tidiness.

As the front door closed behind them, they were enveloped in darkness.

"Sorry," Paige whispered. "Let me turn on a light." She felt her way over to the light switch, trying not to fall.

As she flicked the switch, the room illuminated brightly and she heard someone yell out in surprise. A female someone. Turning her head toward the sound, she froze when she realized what she was seeing. Brandon and Elena sat on the couch, furiously trying to put their clothes back on.

Wait, what? Her brain struggled to catch up to what her eyes were seeing. It didn't make any sense.

"Oh, hey, Paige," Brandon said, looking a little sheepish. "I didn't realize you were coming home so soon."

"I'm, ahhh, I'm sorry," Paige stammered. "I didn't know you…and Elena… I thought you were with Ria."

Elena's face was bright red. "No," Elena said. "I didn't go with her."

That wasn't what Paige had meant by *with*.

Half dressed, Brandon stood and offered his hand to Cara.

"Hi, I'm Paige's roommate, Brandon."

"Lovely to meet you. Cara."

Paige marveled at how unruffled Cara was, walking in on two half-naked strangers, like it was a normal Friday night.

"So… um… yeah, we'll talk about all this later," Paige said to Brandon. "You've clearly been up to some things I had no idea about." He grinned ruefully, like a kid caught sneaking extra Halloween candy.

"Paige, perhaps it might be best if we just call it a night and maybe we can get brunch before I leave for Louisville tomorrow?" Cara smiled as though their evening hadn't been completely ruined.

"I…sure, yes, that would be okay. I'm so sorry. I should have checked in with Brandon first before we came over. I thought he would be *out*." Paige darted a pointed look his way. He bared his teeth apologetically. Elena smiled from the couch but looked too embarrassed to say much.

"It's quite all right."

"At least let me walk you out to your car."

"Of course. Brandon, Elena, I hope to meet you again sometime." Elena nodded her goodbye and Paige followed Cara back out the front door and down the stairs back out to the sidewalk.

"I am so, so sorry," Paige said once they were alone again. "I had no idea. I actually thought Elena was with my friend Ria. I didn't know she was bi, not that that matters, but I guess it makes sense. Ria almost solely dates girls who are bi or straight, but still, wow that's really surprising. I really thought they were together. I mean, not that I care. That's not the point." She stopped and realized she was rambling.

Cara looked at her curiously. "Ah. Your friend Ria, the one you drove up to Chicago with?"

"Yeah, but I swear our lives aren't actually that complicated. It just looks like it."

"It's fine," Cara said. "Really."

"I'm so embarrassed. And now our night is totally ruined."

"I promise, it's fine. And really this is almost better because we still have much to look forward to." She pulled Paige closer and kissed her. Maybe it was the surprise of walking in on Brandon and Elena, but Paige couldn't quite concentrate. Still, it was nice. When they finally pulled apart and Cara climbed into the car, Paige felt dazed, like she didn't even know where she was.

She watched Cara drive away until she turned the corner. Then Paige spun around, ready to kill her roommate for royally messing up her night. As she walked slowly back up the stairs to the apartment, Elena dashed out the door.

"Oh, Elena," Paige started. "You don't have to leave. I'm so sorry. I didn't mean to walk in on you. Really, you should stay."

"I'm getting up early tomorrow anyhow," she said, her cheeks bright pink. "Mila and I have started walking together in the mornings. It's quite nice."

Paige felt a stab of jealously that Elena and Mila were close enough to have morning routines. But then, why shouldn't they? "Okay, well, I'm really sorry to have surprised you like that. Come back any time."

"Thank you," Elena said and then rushed off.

Did she really just tell her to come back any time? God, she was an awkward goober.

She swung the front door open. Brandon was nowhere in sight. "All right, Casanova, get your seducing ass out here!" Brandon popped his head out of his bedroom, an innocent expression on his face. "Yeah, you. Get out here."

Brandon obeyed, plunking himself down on the couch where, just moments ago, he had been caught in a compromising position.

"Spill it," Paige demanded.

"Spill what?"

"You're not funny. How long exactly has this been going on?"

"Well, we've been talking a lot ever since we went up to Chicago. We just clicked, and well… Then we started clicking some more."

"Does Ria know? I thought that she and Elena were… a thing."

Brandon tilted his head back and laughed. "Ha! No way. That's like, ancient history. I thought you knew that. They're just friends now, trust me. And yes, she knows. I'm not sure how much she knows, but she definitely knows we've been hanging out."

Paige's head was swimming. She wasn't sure if it was from the wine or all the new information. She could feel her thoughts recalibrating themselves. That she'd been so wrong was just… hard to wrap her mind around. So all this time, Ria and Elena hadn't been together after all. Why did she feel so relieved?

"I was going to tell you," Brandon continued, "but you pretty much haven't been here at all in the last week."

"I've been working."

"Fair enough, but I didn't have a chance to fill you in on all the dirty details."

Paige picked up a pillow and threw it at him. "You can keep all the dirt to yourself, thanks. I think I need to bleach my eyes out after what I walked in on."

"Aw, we were just talking. You missed all the really good stuff."

"Ew…" she said. "I think that's enough. I'm going to bed. Please feel free to set fire to our sofa."

"Well, wait a minute, little lady," Brandon said, putting on his best dad voice. "I do believe you had someone coming home with you as well. Care to explain?"

"I certainly do not." She tilted her nose up high in the air.

"That was the Chicago lady, right? The one you met about the mural?"

"And so what if it is?"

"I'm impressed. She is..." Brandon let out a piercing whistle. "I mean, nice work, Paige!"

She rolled her eyes. "Goodnight, Brandon."

"Goodnight, lady Casanova."

"Lady Casanova isn't a thing."

"Well, what is? Mata Hari?"

She made a face and turned down the hall. She went into her bedroom and closed the door behind her. Although she was incredibly tired all of a sudden, she lay on her bed, staring up at the ceiling, her thoughts whirling.

CHAPTER SIXTEEN

"Nooo!" Paige grumbled, as Brandon stood over her, shaking her awake. "Too early!"

"Up and at 'em, sunshine. It's Wednesday."

"It's not even light out yet."

"Same as every Wednesday then. So you know you'll complain, ultimately get up, and then be happy you did."

"You have way too much energy for five a.m."

Brandon took an edge of the blanket and began pulling it behind him as he walked out of the room.

"Leaving in ten! Don't forget to hydrate."

Paige lay staring at the ceiling for a few moments, her body demanding that she roll over and immediately go back to sleep. The same as every week. But she glanced down at herself. Yeah, this was why she went to sleep Tuesday nights with her workout gear already on.

"All right," she mumbled. She sat up and grabbed a ponytail holder from her night stand and threw her hair up in a high ponytail. Her socks and shoes sat neatly at foot of the bed. Cracking her neck, she was ready to go in minutes.

"That's my girl." Brandon smiled as she emerged from the bedroom.

"I'm here." She yawned. "Mostly."

Brandon was wide awake, no sign that he'd been out most of the night with Elena and had very little sleep, but Paige had heard him come in around three a.m. She made a mental note to tease him about it once she was awake enough to come up with some witty remarks.

They took down their bikes and once on the street, headed for the War Memorial. The pre-dawn city was quiet, peaceful. This was part of what she loved about Wednesdays, this feeling that she was up and doing something productive before the rest of the city had even had their breakfast. With no traffic, it was only minutes to their destination. Locking their bikes against a railing, they glanced up the stairs at the loosely assembled group.

They'd been meeting up every Wednesday for the last several years, no matter the weather or the season, and Paige was surprised at how much she looked forward to it. People filtered in and out from week to week, but the core group came religiously.

Brandon headed up to check for any newbies. As the time reached five-thirty, he and the other leader, a marathon runner named Sarah, marshaled the troops. They started bouncing on their toes and the group followed suit. The motion helped wake them up and get motivated.

"Good morning!" Brandon yelled.

"Good morning!" the group boomed back.

"Are we good?"

"Fuck yeah!" the group shouted in unison.

"I said are we good?" he yelled louder.

"Fuck yeah!" Paige laughed and bounced along with the group.

A latecomer dashed up the steps and found a place next to her. "Sorry I'm late," Elena whispered, immediately joining in.

Paige caught Brandon's eye and gave him a look that said "oh really?" He hadn't even warned her. And of course, Elena looked like she just walked off the cover of a fitness magazine, her purple-cropped leggings and tight black athletic top showing off the form of her slim body. She, in contrast, was in a T-shirt with the arms chopped out, ventilating her sides and showing off her plain black sports bra. Paige still couldn't believe that Elena and Brandon were together. That was a lot to wrap her mind around.

Brandon gave her a look that said "sorry not sorry" and went back to leading the group. He brought that week's newcomers into the middle of the circle.

Paige nudged Elena, "Better get in there."

The regulars surrounded the newcomers and bounced along with them, learning their names and giving them high fives. This was one of the parts Paige loved, that this group was welcoming to anyone who showed up. Her other friends half-jokingly called it a cult, said there was absolutely no way they would get up that early to work out. She tried to get them to join her, but they just looked at her like she was nuts. She knew if they came, they'd get it. Sure, on paper it sounded like something she would absolutely reject, but starting the day with these happy energetic people made Wednesday one of her favorite days of the week.

The group assembled to hear their instructions for the morning. Brandon and Sarah had decks of cards in their hands.

"There are three stations this morning," Sarah said. "One exercise at each, and you'll draw cards to see how many you'll do. Keep pulling cards until the whistle blows. The first station is jumping jacks. The second is burpees." The group groaned good naturedly. "The third is push-ups. In between each station you'll run to the other side of the memorial, run down the stairs to the street, all the way back up the stairs to the door, and then run to the next station."

"Split up into three groups," Brandon said. "And, go!"

Paige ran for the far group and gathered with a handful of others. Elena followed after her. "I didn't really follow all that," she said.

"That's okay. So, this is the dreaded burpee station. Do you know what burpees are?"

Elena shook her head no.

"You jump down, go into a plank, do a pushup, bring your knees back in, and then jump up to standing with your arms up. That's one. And then you do it all over again."

Elena nodded, her eyes wide.

"Just watch what we do," Paige said.

One of the guys turned over a card. The nine of hearts. "All right, nine burpees."

Paige watched out of the corner of her eye as Elena tried to match their actions. Once each of them counted their nine, they flipped over another card. Seven.

They kept going until they heard the whistle, and then the group took off around the side of the memorial and ran down the steps. Elena seemed to be keeping pace at first, but as Paige began running up the stairs, she could tell that the girl was already winded.

For a moment she felt a little smug. Elena might be gorgeous, but she clearly wasn't used to working out. But that wasn't how this worked. Everyone was welcome, regardless of fitness level. So Paige slowed and ran alongside her, giving her encouraging smiles.

They went through push-ups, ran more stairs, then did jumping jacks. As they passed others in the group they gave high fives and yelled, "nice!" and "you got this!"

When the final whistle blew, telling them they were all done for the day, Elena exhaled loudly and flopped down on the ground.

"How'd it go?" Brandon asked, coming up behind them.

"She did awesome," Paige said.

Elena smiled, still catching her breath.

The group gathered up for their weekly photo on the steps and made silly faces for the camera.

"Thanks Paige," Elena said. "That was very hard. I appreciate you getting me through it."

"Any time. You should have seen me the first time I came. I hurt for days afterward."

"I see why Ria likes you so much."

“Oh please. If she were here she’d run circles around us.”

“Maybe. But you know,” she looked around as though looking for someone listening in. “She never did get over you.”

“What?”

“But you didn’t hear that from me.” She smiled and ran over to Brandon, enveloping him in a sweaty hug.

“Hey Paige,” he called. “You going to breakfast with us?”

She shook her head. She figured she’d let the lovebirds have a little time alone.

Her phone dinged as she rode her bike through the stirring city, the sun peeking out over the rooftops. *What had Elena meant by that?* Once home, she checked the message. Ria. How did she always seem to know when she was thinking about her?

My flight gets in this afternoon. Any chance you’d pick me up? I’d owe you one.

How could she say no to that?

CHAPTER SEVENTEEN

"I can't believe you actually walked in on them," Ria said, once she'd put her bags in Paige's trunk and climbed into the passenger seat. Paige waved at the traffic guard staring them down to make sure they didn't loiter in the pickup lane any longer than possible.

"They told you about that? Oh my god, it was so embarrassing. It was like being back in the college dorms all over again. I haven't walked in on a hookup in years!"

"You should have just sat down right next to them and turned on the TV like it was no big deal."

"I'm sorry," Paige cut in. "Is this weird for you?"

"Huh? Weird why?"

"Because Elena's your ex-girlfriend?"

"From a million years ago."

"Weren't you together for a couple of years? That's got to feel at least a little strange."

"Not really, no. By the end, we were mostly just friends anyway. So breaking up just meant we were only friends. She's really sweet. She just wasn't the one."

"All right. If you say so."

"I say so. And anyhow, isn't it lesbian law that we have to be friends with all of our exes?"

"Ha. They say that, but I haven't really kept up with any of mine." *Well, except for you. If that counts.*

"So what about you, anyway? I hear you're seeing that art lady?"

She felt her face turn bright red and she tried to focus on navigating traffic. "I don't know what that is yet. Elena told you, huh?"

"She had to say something to distract me from teasing her about her and Brandon getting busted."

"Well, she's nice." Paige felt herself growing defensive. "It's still really new. I don't know if it's a thing yet. I'm trying not to worry too much about it and just let whatever happens happen."

Ria laughed. "The Paige I knew wasn't really a relaxed and casual kind of girl, at least when it came to dating."

"Well, shows what you know," she joked. "I'm like so casual now that it's Casual Friday every day."

Ria got quiet and stared out the window. After a few more minutes of silence, Paige glanced over at her, concerned. "Did your trip go well?"

"Yeah, it was good."

"Any solid possibilities?"

"I think so, yeah. Tennessee was definitely interested in me. Virginia I didn't love, even though they were plenty nice. But of course North Carolina would be my first choice. How could it not? I'd learn a ton from their head coach. It'll just depend on what their final offer is, if they make one."

"Well they'd be stupid not to hire you."

Ria lapsed back into silence.

She knew she shouldn't pry, but she pressed on anyway. "I'm sure it feels weird, that you're going to be the coach instead of the player."

"What?" Ria looked confused.

"You seem kind of… lost in thought. I figured maybe it's hard giving up playing and starting to teach up and coming players instead."

"It's not that."

"What is it then?"

"Paige, can you pull over somewhere for a minute?"

"Oh. Um, yeah. Sure. Hold on." She took the next exit and found a truck stop with a large, mostly empty parking lot.

"What's up?"

Ria unbuckled her seatbelt and faced her. "I had a lot of time to think while I was gone. About what I want. Not just from my career but everything. And then I heard that you were starting to see someone, and I realized I had to say something before it got serious and I lost my chance. Because Paige, what I want most…is you."

Paige was stunned. "Me?" She hadn't really believed Elena before, or maybe she'd been afraid to.

"Yes, you."

"What are you talking about?"

"I'm talking about ever since you came into the bike shop a few weeks ago, I haven't stopped thinking about you for a minute."

"Ria… I…"

"Just… hold on. God, I practiced this on the plane and it's not coming out right."

"Ria…"

"I know. I know, we were just starting to be friends again, but it's not what I want. I don't want to be friends. I want more."

"I don't know what to say."

"You haven't even thought about it?"

"I didn't even know it was a possibility. We had just started being friends again and then I thought you were back with Elena, and then…"

"And then you met your art lady. I know. I should have said something earlier, but I wanted to really be sure of my feelings before I went for it and screwed things up all over again. You're worth more than that. I don't want to ruin our friendship, now that we have it back, but I also don't want to ruin the chance if we might have a future as something more."

Paige's thoughts were a muddy, confused swirl. It didn't seem real. Surely, Ria wasn't sitting in front of her in the parking lot of some truck stop saying all this. Not now. Not after everything.

"Ria, I can't… I just, let me think about all this, okay?"

"Yeah, okay. Think about it."

Paige started the car and headed back onto the highway. They rode in silence the rest of the way to the Worths' house. When they got there, Ria grabbed her things quickly from the trunk and leaned into the open window.

"I didn't mean to just throw all that on you. I'm sure it came completely out of nowhere. But when I heard you were starting to see someone, I just… I knew I needed to say it now while I still might have a chance."

Paige nodded, not ready to voice her thoughts.

"Call me or text me when you've had a chance to think about it, okay?"

"Okay," Paige said.

She was tempted to say more, but she didn't have the words yet. Ria looked so nervous, so vulnerable, in a way Paige had rarely seen her. She wanted to tell her it was going to be okay. But they had so much history.

Ria looked like she was going to say something else, but then she stopped herself and instead turned toward the house. Paige sat stunned until Ria disappeared inside.

CHAPTER EIGHTEEN

Paige sat in her car in the driveway, her synapses sending competing signals to her brain. Some told her to turn on the car, peel out of there, and pretend she hadn't heard a word Ria'd just said. The others told her to get out of the car and go find her, right now. She felt a heady mix of emotions building inside her, threatening to spill out. Part of her wanted to rush in and say yes, let's do this. But as she thought over everything that had happened between them, what Ria had done in college and the years she'd lost, she couldn't help it. The emotion that won out was anger. It surprised her at its force.

Enough. I'm not pushing things down any more. She threw open the car door and slammed it shut behind her. Striding up to the house, she steadied herself. She was finally going to get some answers.

Ria was in the kitchen, leaning against the counter and drinking a glass of water.

"How fucking dare you," Paige said. She wasn't going to cry. Hell, maybe she was going to cry. She was past caring.

Ria looked up at her like a startled deer. She looked like she was going to say something, but Paige stopped her. "No. I don't want to hear anything you might have to say right now. How dare you come back into my life when things are going well and try to screw it all up? Goddamn it, Ria. You had your chance. You know you broke my fucking heart, right? Maybe it was over ten years ago but it's not like it's just disappeared from my memory. You treated me like I meant absolutely nothing to you. I was your goddamn best friend. I was supposed to be different. I thought I *was* different. And you had the gall to pretend like you didn't even remember. Like you hadn't said you loved me. Like we hadn't spent the whole night making plans. I was going to come with you to France." Tears poured down her face but she continued.

"I was going to paint and sell art to tourists while you played soccer, and we were going to travel and explore the world together. And then morning came and you pretended not to remember. Like I would believe that. But I just took it. I let you pretend. I didn't force it. Because if you didn't really want me, then it didn't matter anyway.

"But now? Now that we were finally becoming friends again. Now that I was willing to ignore all the years I spent feeling like you tore my heart out. Like I'd lost the person I loved most in the world *and* my best friend. Now you think you can just tell me you have feelings for me? That's not how it works, Ria! I don't care how long ago it was. It might as well have been yesterday. Because you never said you were sorry. You just pretended like it didn't happen, and then you pretended like you didn't even notice that we weren't friends anymore. And I let you. And none of it is okay."

Ria looked at her like she'd been gutted. For a moment, Paige felt guilty, but she stood strong.

"I need you to admit it. That you remembered. That you were just pretending."

Ria breathed. She looked like she was going to cry, and she rarely ever cried. "I remembered. But there was more to it," she said quietly.

"Tell me, then. Tell me why you would do that to me."

Ria took a deep breath. She looked at the floor and then raised her eyes. "I woke up that morning so happy. When I opened my eyes, and you were next to me, it was all I'd ever wanted. You were fast asleep. You know how heavily you sleep, like nothing short of a tornado could wake you? So I got up and went to your kitchen to make coffee and see if there was any food in the fridge. And that's where I found it. Your acceptance letter to UCLA was right on top of the microwave and I read it. It offered you a full scholarship for your MFA. You'd always talked about going to UCLA someday and how amazing their programs were. And there it was, an offer for you to have it. And you hadn't even told me! You let me go on and on about playing soccer in France, and going to camp for the national team, and you talked about coming with me, and I realized you were going to give up your own dreams to follow mine.

"I was so tempted to let you. I thought about putting the letter back, pretending I hadn't seen it, coming back to bed and making more plans for our future together. But then, it dawned on me. I'd be letting you give up everything for me, and what if you regretted it someday? It would be my fault. I knew you wouldn't have thought twice about turning that program down and coming with me. It's the kind of person you were, that you still are. So I got my things. I snuck out. And I made up that stupid excuse about being so drunk I couldn't remember anything. I didn't know what else to do.

"I'm so sorry that I hurt you. I'd rather hurt myself a thousand times than hurt you even once. But don't you see? I did it for a good reason. Look where you are now! Painting giant murals and creating amazing artwork for bands all over the world. If you'd come with me, you probably wouldn't have had all that. It all worked out, in the end, didn't it?"

Ria looked up at Paige, her expression begging for forgiveness, for understanding.

But Paige stared back, furious. She stood, shaking, and finally opened her mouth to speak. "Do you really think you were some kind of hero? That was not your choice to make! It was my life! If I wanted to throw away all my plans and go with you, that was up to me. Even if it was a complete disaster, even if it was stupid and foolish and a total mess. How could you?" Ria started to protest, but Paige kept going.

"Don't. Don't try to defend it. What you did was just as bad as what you let me believe. You lied to me. You hurt me. And you thought you knew what was best for me so you just decided what I should do. And now you want to try again. Have you even grown up at all?"

Tears streamed down Ria's face. She tried to wipe them away, but they kept coming. Paige steeled her heart. She wasn't going to let Ria's pain change her mind. Not after all of this.

"My answer is no, Ria. No. I don't want to date you. I don't even know if we can be friends. I can't be with someone who doesn't let me be equal. Who doesn't respect me enough to even let me make my own choices."

"Paige…I'm sorry."

"I have to go." She spun around and ran for the door. Mila was just coming down the stairs as she passed.

"Paige?"

"I'm sorry, Mila," was all she could get out.

She got in her car and started driving. Halfway home, she had to pull over. By the side of the road, she broke down. Tears poured out, all the things she thought she'd gotten over, all the dashed hopes. It was even worse, she thought. Ria did want her, but she wanted to make all the decisions for both of them. Sure, Ria thought she was doing the right thing, but Paige didn't care about the reason. It was like it was all happening again.

She cried until she couldn't cry anymore, and once it finally passed, she pulled back onto the road and headed home.

CHAPTER NINETEEN

"Hello? Earth to Paige?" Brandon waved his hand in front of her eyes.

She sat at the kitchen table, staring blankly at the window, her coffee gone cold in front of her.

"Oh, hey."

"Are you okay?"

"Yeah. I'm fine. Just…thinking." Ria had called so many times that she'd finally turned her phone off. She didn't want to talk to her.

"Can I do anything?"

"No. I'm okay. What's up?" She looked up at him and realized that he was practically glowing with happiness. At least one of them was happy. That was something.

"Elena and I would like to invite you to join us at the Worths' for dinner tomorrow night. She's cooking something special as her way to thank everyone for putting her up and making her feel at home."

"Oh, Brandon, I don't know if I can do dinner..." The last thing she wanted was to see Ria right now. The anger had settled into a heavy mix of emotions that she hadn't yet parsed out.

"Come on, she really wants you to come."

"She barely knows me."

"Okay, well, I want you to come. I'm really crazy about her and I want you to come hang out with us."

She sighed. She thought about making up an excuse about last-minute changes needed for the mural. Normally she would tell Brandon all her troubles, vent and yell about Ria and what she'd done. They would psychoanalyze the roller coaster of emotions running through her head. But he just looked so much like an eager puppy that she couldn't bring him down. He was a good friend. She owed him this.

"Fine," she said. "What can I bring?"

She wasn't sure how she was going to be in the same room with Ria. It had been a week and she couldn't stop thinking about Ria's explanation for why she'd done it. Looking back now, it made sense, the puzzle pieces now in place. She'd tried to do the right thing, but she'd botched it. She kept hearing Ria's words before that, too, saying she wanted to try again. It was both too much, and too little too late. She was still ignoring her calls and texts. Cara had been texting her too, and she'd been responding, but something had changed. It was like the air had gone out of it and she was having trouble mustering the enthusiasm to pursue her. Leave it to Ria to quash the excitement she'd been feeling for another woman—finally, when she met someone who she might actually like, who actually spoke her language. It was so hard to meet someone in Indianapolis. Not that there weren't any women there, but it was a relatively small dating pool, and she felt like she always had to make so many compromises if things got serious.

Maybe she should just move. Her dad didn't need her here anymore, and there wasn't really anything tying her down. She could work from anywhere. She wasn't great at making friends, but she'd manage. She had Brandon here, but now he was in love and things were bound to change.

She was going up to Chicago the next day to start painting the mural. Maybe she should think about moving there? It was close enough that she could come back and visit her dad. She liked the city. Maybe she would look around while she was there and see if she could find any decent apartments. She'd be sad to leave Brandon, but he could come up and visit too.

I just have to get through this one dinner. Then I'll get started on my new life. Not a whole new life. Just new in the parts I'm lacking.

She decided to wear a costume, to pretend to be someone else. At the back of her closet she had several dresses. She'd bought them and then always found excuses not to wear them. Dresses always made her feel like not quite herself, and today, that's what she wanted.

She chose a knee-length sundress covered in sunflowers. It looked happy, and she hoped the vibrant color would change her mood. She plaited her hair into a long, pale braid that hung over one shoulder, and she carefully outlined her eyes with a navy pencil and curled her eyelashes. Adding a dash of mascara and pulling on some sandals, she stood in front of the mirror. She looked different, but good, she thought. This Paige could handle one awkward dinner.

At the Worths' house, she stood in front of the door, putting it off as long as she could. She felt like she should ring the doorbell for some reason, though she hadn't done so since she was a little kid. She was still standing in front of the door when it flew open in front of her.

Brandon grinned. "Hey! I thought I heard a car. Come on in!"

He grabbed her by the wrist and led her into the kitchen where, just a week ago, she and Ria had come to verbal blows. But now it was a hotbed of activity and Elena crouched over the stove, taking out a pan of something that smelled heavenly. Pots simmered on the burners and a tray of fruits and vegetables sat on the counter.

"I'm so glad you could make it," Elena said, grinning. She pulled the oven mitts off her hands and gave Paige a kiss on each cheek. "We are almost ready!"

"Paige, would you mind taking that tray into the living room?" Brandon asked, nodding at the fruits and veggies.

"Um...sure," she said. She guessed she would have to go in there eventually.

"We'll call you to dinner!" Elena said.

Paige carried the tray in and stopped short when she realized the only other people there were Ria, Mila, and Henry. She'd imagined the entire family being there, but of course, they'd all returned to their own cities or they were at home with their families. So it was to be just the six of them. Her heart beat just a little harder, but she steeled herself. This was for Brandon, she reminded herself, and he deserved every bit of happiness, even if he'd found it with her ex-best friend's ex-girlfriend. Who was she to judge? Elena seemed sweet, and hell, if she'd put up with Ria for two years, she must have a lot of patience.

Ria was talking to her dad when Paige walked in, and when she looked up, she smiled, almost apologetically.

"Um, where can I put this down?" Paige asked.

"Over on the coffee table, dear," Mila said. "Elena is certainly going all out tonight for this dinner. Come sit over here by me." She patted the seat next to her on the couch.

Paige sat, careful to cross her legs. She remembered why she didn't wear dresses more often. They made simple tasks just a little bit harder.

She wondered if Mila and Henry had noticed the tension between her and Ria. She didn't know what Ria had told them after the day they'd argued, and she definitely didn't want to talk about it.

"So, Mila, tell me about the book you're working on. How's it going?"

"Ugh. I have a new editor," she said, waving a hand in frustration. "She's only twenty-five! Can you believe it. How am I supposed to take her seriously when she's barely lived?"

"Oh no. Is she trying to make you write in emojis?" Paige joked.

"You kid, but just wait! I heard about a man who wrote an entire novel on Twitter."

"I'm sure that's bound to be a classic," Ria joined in, coming over and sitting on the arm of the couch. Paige gave her a tight smile, the best she could manage.

"Are they sending you on a book tour this time?" Paige asked.

"They want me to do some podcasts. And they'll definitely send me to the romance book festival."

"I didn't even know there was such a thing."

"You should go with her," Ria said. "It's fascinating. Thousands of people who love romance novels so much that they want to go to a convention about them. And they totally love my mom. People wait in the longest lines to get her autograph."

"It's true. My hand starts to cramp after a while, but I certainly can't complain. So many people write novels that no one reads. I try to remember to be grateful."

Brandon poked his head into the room. "Dinner is served."

Paige breathed a sigh of relief. At least now she could keep her hands busy, and how long could dinner take, maybe an hour? She was well on her way through the evening, and there was a light at the end of the tunnel.

The table looked amazing. It had been set with bright red placemats and a table runner. The good white china was set neatly at each place. Elena beamed proudly as the family walked in. Henry sat at his usual place at one end, with Mila to his left. Paige glanced at Brandon for direction and he just shrugged, as though to say anywhere was fine. But before she could grab a seat away from Ria, Brandon pulled out a chair for Elena and sat beside her. There was no other choice than to sit between Ria and Mila. She plastered a smile on her face, and sat down.

One thing she had always loved about meals with the Worths was they always held hands and said something thankful before they ate. She chalked it up to Mila's Catholic upbringing, but it didn't feel oppressively religious. Today, Elena asked if she could say the blessing.

"I am so thankful that you have welcomed me into your family over the past several weeks. This truly does feel like my second home. Mila and Henry, you have been so kind to me. Ria, you have been a wonderful friend. Paige, I am so glad to call you a new friend. And Brandon…" She looked at him, her eyes full of joy. "You make me so happy."

He stood next to her. "We were going to wait until after the meal to make a toast, but I just can't wait. Elena, can we please just tell them now?" She nodded. "Everyone, we asked you to dinner tonight to celebrate with us. I've asked Elena to marry me."

"And I said yes." Elena looked at him, her eyes shining.

"Oh my god!" Mila said. "This is so wonderful!" Her eyes teared up. "I am so happy for you two."

Paige realized her mouth was hanging open. She pulled it shut. She was truly speechless. They'd barely known each other a month. But she looked at Brandon and Elena, and they looked so truly happy that she pushed any concerns away and decided to just support whatever was happening.

"Did you know about this?" she whispered to Ria, forgetting for a moment that she wasn't speaking to her.

"Not exactly, but I had an inkling."

"Congratulations," Henry said. "You make a splendid couple."

Brandon kissed Elena and turned back to the family. "Okay, so now we eat!"

The meal went by in a blur. When Brandon got up to get another bottle of wine from the kitchen, Paige joined him. The minute they were out of sight, she punched him in the arm as hard as she could. "I can't believe you didn't tell me."

"We just told you."

"Well, still. I can't believe it. You're getting married! I didn't think you ever wanted to get married."

"She's… She's just it. I know it's a cliché, but I've never felt like this about anyone. And I know it seems totally insane to get engaged when we haven't known each other that long, but I know I'm going to be this crazy about her for the rest of my life."

"Oh my god, you're a total sap. But I'm so happy for you."

"Oh! I forgot the other part! Grab your wine and come back in for a minute."

She eyed him warily. "What else is there?"

"You'll see."

She trailed behind him back into the dining room.

"Everyone!" he announced. "We forgot to tell you the other part!"

"Oh!" Elena said, standing. "We did! I got so distracted about the engaged part that I forgot the other news."

"How can there be more news?" Ria asked.

"Well," Brandon said, "due to the fact that I love Elena so much, and due to our idiotic visa restrictions, Elena and I are getting married…"

"In two weeks!" Elena shouted.

"Oh my god," Paige said.

"Oh my god is right," Ria agreed. "Seriously, only two weeks?"

"Honestly, we thought about just doing it this week," Elena said, "but we know Paige is going up to Chicago to paint, and we really want her there. My family is back in Spain, and we'll go there once we're married so they can meet Brandon. But since they can't come here, we want all of you to be there."

"We're just going to go down to the courthouse," Brandon said.

"Certainly not!" Mila said with an authoritative tone.

"Mila," Henry murmured. "It's their lives."

"What I mean is that you're not going to the courthouse. We'll plan something for you. Just leave it to me, dears. Well, to us."

"Mr. and Mrs. Worth," Elena said, "would you be willing to give me away?"

"Of course, love," Mrs. Worth said, clearly overjoyed at the prospect.

"And Paige, will you be my best man?" Brandon asked. "You don't have to wear a suit."

"Ria, I want you to be my maid of honor!" Elena said.

"Am I allowed to wear a suit?" Ria joked.

"Will you do it?" Brandon asked.

"Of course," Paige said.

"I'd love to," said Ria.

So it was settled. In two weeks, Brandon and Elena were getting married. Paige found herself being swept up in the romance of it, even if her practical side said it was crazy.

CHAPTER TWENTY

If there was one thing Indy was really lacking, it was decent public transportation. Paige would have loved to live without owning a car. Hers was so old that it always made her nervous on long trips. She'd decided not to take it to Chicago. Instead she bought a ticket on the MegaBus, the double-decker bus with a direct route from Indianapolis. This way, she didn't have to drive and instead she could veg out, listen to music, nap, and let her thoughts drift while someone else piloted her there. Once she arrived, the Metro could take her the rest of the way to Cara's studio.

She was nervous to see her again. The last time they'd seen each other they'd almost…but then Brandon and Elena…and it had ended so abruptly. That was two weeks ago, but it somehow felt even longer, especially after Ria's surprise announcement and their ensuing blowup. With all of that, she was actually a little nervous to see Cara again and see if they would pick up where they left off.

Cara had turned her designs into transparencies, and at dusk they were going to project them onto the wall and start painting the outline. That process would take a few days of working from dusk until dawn, and once the whole outline was done, they could start filling it in during the daytime. Paige was prepared to be extremely tired, but it wouldn't be the first time. She couldn't wait to get started.

She watched as the graffiti sped by through the windows of the Metro. Soon she'd be doing her own graffiti. She wondered if anyone would tag over it. Hopefully people would like it, but that was no guarantee that it would survive unscathed.

Soon she was back at the gallery, just like the first time, but a little more at home now. She wasn't startled by the darkness of the entryway. The work she'd seen last time was now being taken down and prepared for transport to wherever it would show next or live with whoever had purchased it. She peeked around the corner to Cara's office and was surprised not to see her there.

"Oh, hi!" a young man's voice piped up behind her. "You must be Paige."

She turned, surprised.

"I'm Ms. Williams' assistant, Trevor."

"Hi Trevor. Is Cara here?"

"She had a meeting up north, but she said to tell you that she'll meet you at the project site at one. So you've got plenty of time to grab some lunch."

Paige wondered why Cara hadn't just told her herself that she wasn't going to be there, but she knew she hadn't been all that responsive lately. She'd just had so much to think about.

"Oh, um. Okay. Sure. I'll see her there. Will you tell her to call me if she gets done sooner?"

"Of course."

She spent the next two hours checking into her bed & breakfast and walking through downtown Chicago, just enjoying the sheer density of people. Even though she was surrounded, she felt completely unobserved, like she could do anything—jump, yell, bust a dance move—and people would just shrug and keep walking.

She finally made her way over to the building that would soon display her mural. Cara was already there, talking animatedly to a man in a hard hat, standing next to the cherry picker that would lift Paige high up in the air to paint lines on cement several stories above the ground.

Cara smiled when she saw her and waved her over. "Paige, I'd like you to meet Daniel Forcliff. He's going to keep an eye on your safety while you're up there, and he's also the only one allowed to move this fine piece of machinery."

"My new best friend," Paige said, cheerily.

"You better believe it," Daniel replied. "I'll be helping you up, down, and sideways for the next several days."

"So you're saying, if I have to go to the bathroom..."

"You'll have to signal me or take a chamber pot up there with you."

"Good to know, Dan, good to know."

"Well ladies, if we're going to get started soon, I'd better do some last checks."

"Thank you, Daniel," Cara said as he strode away.

"Now Paige, we'll have some media stopping by to get a photo of your first brushstroke and to ask you a few questions. You're all right with that?"

"Oh, um, yes, of course. I'd be happy to."

Paige couldn't help but wonder why Cara was so businesslike. Was it because she was in work mode right now or had she lost interest? Paige regretted not having been more responsive. Had she already messed this up? Maybe it was all fine and Cara was just doing her job like an actual professional.

Within the hour, a reporter from a local weekly stopped by. She asked a few quick questions of Paige before moving on to Cara. Soon a slew of officials arrived. It looked like everyone who had ever touched the project in any way, or even been in the same room as someone who had, arrived. It's too late to be nervous, Paige thought.

When the media was set up, all of the dignitaries chose a paintbrush, dipped them in a little paint and held them up carefully for a photo. The cameras clicked, flashed, and whirred, and Paige tried her hardest to smile and not blink. Then the group disbanded, and Paige climbed up into the cherry picker and secured the harness around her waist.

"Up we go," she said to no one in particular, and she gave Daniel the thumbs-up. He signaled back and the machine began to climb.

Paige worked from eight p.m. until eleven, when she needed to take a break to use the bathroom and warm up a little. She pushed the button on the walkie-talkie Dan had given her.

"Lunar module to ground," she said. "Come in, ground."

"Oh, we have a comedienne," came the crackling reply.

"Operation help-I-need-to-pee is in full effect. Do you copy?"

"Copy, art nerd. Hold tight and I'll have you back on the ground in just a moment."

The coffee shop next door had given them a key to the side door, and the minute she was on the ground, Paige dashed inside to use the bathroom.

When she came back out, Cara was talking to Dan. Had she been there the whole time? Surely not. Paige stood back, appraising the section of the mural she'd been outlining. A moment later, Cara joined her.

"Hey, lady," Paige said. "Here to check out the progress?"

"That and to bring you something hot to drink. I know it's getting warmer, but it still gets a little chilly at night. I'm sure the higher up you go, the colder it gets, with the wind and all." She handed Paige a travel mug, holding one of her own in her other hand. "It's black tea with orange."

"It smells wonderful," Paige said, holding the warm mug between her hands.

"And it has a little caffeine to give you a boost. How are you holding up so far?"

"I'm making some progress. And it's fun getting to use such large brushes."

"Big art, big tools."

"That should be embroidered on a pillow somewhere."

"Maybe I'll branch out from the gallery. Start my own line of pillows with cheeky sayings."

"I know I'd buy at least two."

Cara smiled at her, and they lapsed into silence, looking up at the spot-lit wall and the dark lines Paige had spent the past few hours painting in one corner.

Cara reached an arm around her waist. Paige leaned into it, ready to feel the butterflies leap out again. She waited, but after a few moments she realized that they weren't there. Where had they gone? Cara was still beautiful, still brilliant and thoughtful, but she could tell that something had changed.

Cara must have felt it too. "Paige," she said. "I like you. And I'd love to work with you again. But I think that we're simply going to be great friends, don't you?"

"I'm so sorry. I don't know what happened." She gave Cara a pained smile.

"Some things last longer than others, but we just appreciate them for what they are. If they're meant to be, I think we know."

She felt guilty. Cara was an absolute catch, and here she was, letting her drift away. *Damn it, Ria.* She'd managed to get in her head after all.

"Shall we toast?" Cara asked, raising her tea. "To leaving your mark on the city, literally and figuratively."

"And to making art, and making new friends." They leaned against one another, gazing at the brush strokes just beginning to take shape, lit by the glow of the projector in the night.

CHAPTER TWENTY-ONE

If only she'd driven, Paige thought. She could shave time off her route home. Even only a few minutes would mean she'd get there sooner. Ever since Cara had graciously let her go, her thoughts had only been on Ria, as she spent the long night hours alone in the cherry picker.

She finally knew what she wanted. She'd thought about calling her, having this conversation by phone, but it seemed too huge, too important not to speak to her face to face. She needed to see her expressions and body language, feel the air between them as she told her that she loved her too, that she'd never stopped.

If she wasn't already too late.

But instead of hurtling forward in her car, she was back on the MegaBus, full to capacity this time so she had to squish in next to a man, instead of stretching out across two seats like she had on the way up. Napping to pass the time was out of the question, as her seatmate had no qualms about holding heated conversations over the telephone. He shouted through the phone as though he could strangle the person on the other end with just the force of his voice. She tried not to listen, but it was nearly impossible.

It was going to be a long ride, and the bus was too full for her to pick up and move.

She tried to imagine how she would start when she saw Ria again. "Ria, you're right." *No.* "Ria, I'm sorry." *No.* "Ria, I'm not sorry. You're the one who should be sorry, but we're past all that so let's just do this." Surely by the time she got home she'd figure out the right words.

Between her seatmate's shouting, and the bus's full capacity making her feel a little claustrophobic, Paige squirmed for the entire ride. She was grateful when they finally arrived at her stop outside of the Indianapolis City Market and she could breathe again.

But she was no closer to knowing what to say.

Mila had made her promise to text when she was close to home. She'd found outfits for the wedding, and she needed Paige to come over to the house to see if her dress needed any last-minute adjustments. Paige could see Henry's car waiting in a parking spot just outside the market, ready to take her there.

She'd wanted to have a chance to go home, shower, and make herself look nice before seeing Ria again, but there was no time. Running a hand through her hair, this would have to do.

She squinted at the car before she made her way over. Was Ria sitting inside? No, it was only Henry. She had another twenty-minute car ride before they reached the Worth house. She wasn't sure her heart could take it.

Henry saw her and jogged over to the bus, insisting on helping her with her bag. Paige marveled at the gray in his hair. In her mind, he'd always be the dad in his mid-thirties, running the length of the soccer field alongside the kids, cheering them on. But he was getting older. And that must mean she was too.

"How was Chicago?" he asked as he drove them toward the house. "Was the city windy?"

Paige laughed courteously. "It actually was, mostly when I was up three stories and trying to paint in the middle of the night."

"Mila showed me the pictures. It looks beautiful. We're talking about taking a trip up there to see it, and Mila wants to see a show. *Wicked*, I think."

"She would love that. The show, I mean. So how have the wedding preparations been? I'm sure Mila has been a flurry of activity."

"You have no idea. She's been absolutely loving it. You know she loves to plan a party, so a wedding in two weeks? Challenge accepted."

"Where did they decide to have the wedding?"

"Well, I don't want to get in trouble by telling you too much myself. All I'll say is, the plans are very much a combination of Mila, Brandon and Elena, and some wacky ideas from Ria."

"Fair enough. I'll let Mila give me the full rundown."

The moment they walked in the front door, Mila was calling for them. Paige barely had time to drop her bags before being ushered into the living room, which had been transformed by what looked like the full inventory of a craft store.

"Oh wow," Paige said, her eyes wide as she took everything in.

"Henry thinks I may have gone a little overboard. But everything has a purpose, if there is enough time, of course."

"I thought this was a small wedding."

"Well, it is. Though I may have invited a few friends to the reception. We want this to be memorable for Elena and Brandon, don't we?"

Paige smiled. "I'm sure whatever you do, it will be memorable."

Mila stood back, looking Paige up and down. "I think the dress will fit fine. I didn't have your size, so I had to guess, but I'm good at guessing these things."

Mila grabbed a garment bag lying across the back of an armchair and pressed it into Paige's arms.

"Take this up to Ria's room and try it on, and then come down and show me."

"Is Ria here?"

"She's out with Elena getting her bridal gown altered. Somehow she managed to find something straight off the rack that just needed a few little tweaks. I'm not sure when they'll be back, but Ria certainly won't mind if you use her room."

"I can just use the bathroom..."

"Don't be silly. Ria's closet has that full-length mirror so you can see how everything looks."

Mila hustled her out of the room and up the stairs. Paige hoped Elena had known about Mila's love of planning things before she announced the wedding. It was certainly too late now to elope.

Paige paused at Ria's door. When was the last time she'd been in here? It must have been sometime during college, visiting home for a weekend or a holiday. She felt like she was intruding on Ria's private space, even though Ria hadn't lived here for years. Still, her things were here, and she'd been sleeping here for the past month. It felt strange to go in without her. But it would be worse not to follow Mila's instructions, so she went inside.

She pushed the door closed behind her. It bounced off the door frame slightly instead of clicking closed, but she instantly forgot anything else as she looked at the wall over Ria's bed.

There hung Paige's painting, the one she'd shown in Florence during grad school and had immediately regretted selling. The one of the doll-like versions her and Ria that she'd painted while the wound was still fresh, with the Ria doll's hand pulling Paige's heart from her chest. How... How did it get there?

Tears welled in her eyes as she looked at the lost piece, which had been here all along. She barely registered the sound of the door opening behind her.

"I've always loved that painting," Ria said quietly, just behind her. "Even though it's pretty brutal." Paige spun around, a look of confusion on her face.

"How did you...where..." she sputtered.

Ria looked up at the painting. "I heard about your show from a mutual friend of ours. And I thought, you were in Europe. Maybe it was a sign. Since you were so close, I had to see you."

"Barcelona isn't really that close to France," Paige interrupted. "I know, I wanted to go there during my trip but I didn't have time between classes."

"Okay. It was something like ten hours on the train, but that didn't seem like very long compared to an ocean in between us. Anyway, I didn't care. I found out where your show was, and when I got there it was night, and I could see you through the window. I wanted to go in, but you looked so happy, and I chickened out. I waited until you left. They were just about to close up, but they let me look around first. And I saw this painting. I felt like I got stabbed in the gut, because I knew it was you and me."

"Ria…"

"Even though it was a literal picture of how much I hurt you, I still had to have it. So I bought it, and I made them promise the sale would be anonymous. I didn't want to hurt you anymore. That's when I knew I was letting you go. For good. If I did that to you, if I made you feel the way you had to feel to paint like that, I didn't deserve to be in your life."

"And so you brought it home and hung it on the wall?"

"I asked Mom to hang it up here. I didn't exactly want it hanging in my house where anyone who visited me would see a version of me ripping out someone's heart. I didn't want to be reminded every day of what happened to us. But I liked knowing it was here. It hurt but it reminded me of you."

"I never meant for you to see it."

"I know."

Paige realized she was still holding the dress, and she dropped it on the bed. She turned back to Ria.

"Do you think some things are too broken to fix?" she asked.

"Some things, maybe. But not us. We're resilient, you and me. We've lived whole lives in between who we were then and who we are now. I think we're better now, smarter, but we're still ourselves. You're still the one I love deep down in the middle of my heart. If you can forgive me, if we can give ourselves a real chance, I know we could make it." Ria looked up at her, watching her expression. "But what do you want? Because whatever it is, that's what I want too. No more deciding for you. This time, it's your choice."

Paige looked at the painting. She looked at Ria. She listened to what her heart called out for. It wanted Ria. It had always wanted her.

She took a deep breath and crossed the space between them. "You," she said. "I want you."

Ria gave her a brilliant smile, her whole face lighting up. Paige couldn't help but return it. They stood there, grinning at one another, letting the moment wash over them. Paige pulled Ria close and met her lips, closing her eyes and giving in to what she thought she'd never have again. This was the woman she wanted to spend her whole life with. She knew that for sure.

A knock at the door surprised them. "Paige?" Mila called through the mostly-closed door. "How does the dress fit?"

They jumped apart, startled. Ria started to giggle and Paige shot her a look. If Ria started laughing, she knew that would set her off. Apparently making out in her girlfriend's childhood bedroom meant no matter how old they got, they were still in constant danger of being busted.

Paige glanced down at the untouched dress still lying in its bag on the bed. "It's great, Mila!" It was too late now if it wasn't, anyhow.

"Are you sure? I can take it in a little if you need."

"No, it's perfect. Thank you so much." Ria wrapped her arms around Paige and held her tight as their bodies shook with suppressed laughter.

"All right then. You should probably head home to get ready. Just a few hours left before the big event!"

"Yes, Mila!"

"And Ria?"

Ria coughed. "Um, yeah Mom?"

"It's about time you two figured it out. I thought I'd never get to turn this room into my yoga studio."

CHAPTER TWENTY-TWO

Paige left with a promise to Ria that they would pick up later where they'd left off. Henry offered to drive her, but to keep him from having to go back and forth she insisted on taking an Uber back. She'd go home, get ready, and meet them for the ceremony downtown.

When she walked in the door to her apartment, she heard cursing coming from Brandon's room.

"Everything all right in there?"

He emerged and she couldn't help but laugh when she saw him. He was in a button-down shirt, vest, and…gym shorts. "Paige, thank god."

"I don't think Elena is going to approve of your outfit. And I definitely know Mila will have some things to say about it."

"It's seasonal," he said with a straight face. "Apparently tying a bow tie is the most difficult thing in America. How did I manage to get through my whole life without having to do this?"

"Let me look at this," Paige said, taking the bow tie. She looped it around his neck and easily fashioned the fabric into a bow.

"Now how the hell did you know how to do that?"

"YouTube," she said. "The font of all knowledge."

"Remind me again why we didn't just elope?"

"Because you told Mila about it? Sorry, but at that point it was all out of your hands. So just stand back and let Hurricane Mila do her thing."

"She's actually been awesome," Brandon admitted. "You know my folks and I aren't close…that whole leaving the church thing… So it's nice to have a kind of surrogate family."

"They're good at that," Paige agreed. "It's like they just have so much love that they're happy to share it with those of us who need more."

"That's a good way to describe them."

"So, are you ready to get hitched? I mean, once you put on pants, of course."

"You know what? I really am. And you realize, in a roundabout way, you made this happen."

"A very roundabout way. In that I had no idea it was happening."

"But still. I'm grateful. And also, a little afraid of what Mila has planned for us."

"God help us all. It's going to be fabulous."

With not much time left to waste, Paige showered quickly and blow-dried her hair, using a round brush for some curl. Mascara, a little eyeliner, and some lip gloss rounded out the look. She didn't want to pile it on for a daytime wedding, but she wanted to look nice. This was the first time she and Ria would see each other and know that a future together was real.

In her bedroom, she unzipped the garment bag and pulled out the dress. It was beautiful. The long, pale gray, almost silver pleated dress fell to her ankles. It fit perfectly and its halter neckline showed off her arms and much of her back. She found a pair of heels in the back of the closet and added a few silver bangles to her wrists. Looking in the mirror on her wall, she smiled in approval. Not bad.

Stepping out into the living room, Brandon whistled. He looked handsome in his suit.

"We clean up all right, don't we?" he said.

"Are you ready for this?

"You know, I really am."

The ceremony had been Ria's idea. Of course. Elena had liked the idea of getting married along the canal downtown, but apparently, that required getting a permit from the city, which would take time they didn't have. Ria had not been willing to give up, though.

And that's why Brandon and Paige were hiding in her car in a parking spot around the corner from the fountain, in their formalwear, waiting for the signal.

"This is insane," Paige giggled.

"I feel like we're about to rob a bank," Brandon agreed.

Just then, their phones buzzed.

Go go go! said Ria's text.

Paige and Brandon leapt out of the car and ran-walked down the sidewalk, around a building, and down the stairs to where Ria and Benji were waiting by the fountain. Benji had cleaned up nicely for the occasion, wearing a navy suit, his long hair tied back. When Mila had told her that he'd been ordained online to perform the ceremony, Paige had to laugh. It was perfect.

But it was Ria who took her breath away. Suddenly, she understood that expression. Ria hadn't been kidding about wearing a suit. She was dressed in a gray, fitted, three-piece that closely matched Paige's dress, with a white and gray-striped bow tie at her neck. Her hair was swept loosely back from her face in a pompadour. And the finishing touch: a sweep of dark black eyeliner and perfect red lipstick. Ria could have been featured in any fashion magazine, and Paige felt like she couldn't have spoken if she'd needed to. But there was no time to swoon.

They stood in formation, Benji in the middle with his script in a book, Brandon to one side, his hands folded together. Paige stood behind Brandon, and Ria was opposite on the bride's side. A moment later, Mila and Henry emerged from behind a monument.

"Ready?" Mila called.

"So ready!" Brandon returned.

Mila and Henry joined the group and took places next to Ria and Paige. Amelia emerged with a camera to capture the moment. Benji pulled out his phone, and pushed play, and the wedding march began.

Elena walked out from her hiding spot around the corner of the building and strode slowly toward the group, her long white lace dress hugging her through the bodice then flowing gracefully to the ground. Her eyes locked on Brandon's, and they looked as happy as anyone had a right to be.

Benji kept the ceremony short, but it was beautiful. They had just said "I do" and exchanged rings when they saw a police officer walking down the canal.

"I declare you man and wife!" Benji shouted. "Quick, kiss her and run!"

Brandon and Elena embraced and seemed not to care one bit that their party was about to get busted.

Ria hooted and everyone cheered.

"Ahem," Ria coughed, after the kiss had gone on for a while. "You guys, maybe we should head to a secondary location? I'm sure you can find no shortage of other places to kiss."

The police officer was getting closer, and he did not look particularly amused.

Elena let out a shriek and grabbed Brandon's hand, and they ran off in the opposite direction.

"We'll see you at the theatre!" Mila called. "Come on, Henry." They took off as well, followed closely by Benji and Amelia. The police officer began to pick up speed, seeming to realize that if people were running from the police, there was probably a reason.

"Go, Paige!" Ria said. "I'll distract him while you all get away."

"No way," Paige said. "I'm sticking with you."

Ria gave her a look she couldn't read and then smiled. "All right, here goes." She turned to the policeman. "Good afternoon, officer."

He scowled. "You do know that you need a permit to get married here, don't you? I assume you do since everyone just mysteriously ran away."

"Oh no, do we?" Paige asked, feigning innocence.

"There's a fine for not having a permit." He pulled out a pad and pen, ready to write them a citation. "What are your names? We can start with you."

"Ria Worth. But really, it's all my fault, so I'm happy to pay the fine. It was all my idea, you see."

"Wait." He looked up at her curiously. "Ria Worth, the soccer player?"

"That's me."

"Hmm. My daughter loves you. She plays soccer too."

"Really? What's her name?"

"Emily. She's ten. She's going to be so excited to hear I met you."

"You know, I'd be happy to sign something for her. Regardless of whether you give me a ticket or not," she added hastily.

The officer hesitated. "Well, I guess you all didn't hurt anything. Just, you know, next time you want to get someone married here, get permission first."

"Absolutely."

The officer pulled out a notepad, and Ria scribbled: *To Emily, who loves the game like I do—keep on kicking A! Love, Ria Worth.*

Smiling as he read it, the officer nodded, then began walking away, as though he'd never seen anything in the first place.

"The power of celebrity," Paige whispered.

"It definitely has its perks," Ria whispered back.

Once the officer passed out of view, they nearly collapsed in a pile on a nearby bench.

"That was a wedding like none other I've ever been to," Paige said.

"But fun, you have to admit."

"Definitely fun."

"So... I guess we should get to the reception. Can you believe Mom managed to convince the owner of the Fountain Square Theater to let us have it up on the roof? They never let people do things up there."

"If anyone could convince them, Mila could. He's probably a secret fan of her books."

"You'd be surprised how many people are."

They were tempted to stop by Paige's to really reconnect, but they knew there would be hell to pay with Mila if they showed up too late. That didn't stop them from steaming up the car windows as they made out like teenagers inside.

The dance party had already started on the rooftop by the time they arrived. The place was packed. Paige wasn't entirely sure who all the people were, but Mila had certainly thrown an unbelievable party. A DJ had set up on one side and drinks flowed liberally from the bar on the other.

Paige managed to catch Brandon's eye as she walked in, holding Ria's hand. Her gave her a self-satisfied smirk, and she shrugged and stuck out her tongue. He nodded his approval and turned back to his new wife.

The day turned to dusk, and the dusk turned to night, and they drank and they danced.

She looked at Ria, and in that moment, she was as sure as she'd ever been. She wanted to spend the rest of her life with this woman. Ria looked back at her, and Paige knew she felt the same way.

"So," Ria whispered. "Is this a good time to tell you I got an offer from North Carolina?"

"And what did you tell them?"

"I told them I had to talk to someone first before I accepted."

"You did?"

"I wasn't going to screw it up again, if there was any chance. If you say no, I won't go. I'll find something here or we can go anywhere you want. What do you think?"

"I think I'm going to like it there."

"Are you sure?"

"As sure as I've been about anything in my whole life."

They wrapped their arms around each other and swayed to the music, looking out at the city spread out around them. Wherever they were heading, this time they were going there together.

Bella Books, Inc.

Women. Books. Even Better Together.

P.O. Box 10543
Tallahassee, FL 32302

Phone: 800-729-4992
www.bellabooks.com